KV-575-097

WITHDRAWN
FROM STOCK

1

THE envelope was white, plain and expensive. There were no markings on it. Florence Digby laid it on the desk in front of me.

"There's a messenger outside," she announced. "He's been told to wait for an answer."

I looked at her enquiringly, but she merely shrugged. Ripping open the envelope, I took out a folded sheet of heavy white linen notepaper. Inside the fold were five one-hundred-dollar bills, mint fresh. There was a typed message on the paper. It read

A courier is required to deliver some valuable property. The job should take three hours. The fee will be $5,000. If you are interested, tell the messenger there is no answer. You will then receive telephone

1

Cork City Library
WITHDRAWN
FROM STOCK

instructions. If you are not interested, retain $200 for your expenses and return the rest in a sealed envelope to the messenger. You will then hear nothing further.

And that was it.

I read it twice, and looked at the money three times. Florence waited expectantly. Without comment I passed her the note, and she scanned it quickly.

"You'll refuse, naturally."

"Oh, why will I?"

She frowned.

"Because it's obviously crooked. They probably have a suitcase full of heroin or stolen jewellery. Something awful like that."

I shook my head. People in that kind of business do not send messengers with typed notes.

"I don't think so, Florence. This isn't the way they operate. Oh," I carried on, since she was obviously about to interrupt, "I don't doubt that it's something unusual, something the police would like to know about. But I'm not going to turn it down without knowing more about it. Let's have a look at this courier."

In the outer office a shaven-headed kid leaned against the wall, picking at his nails. There seemed to be pieces of metal hanging all over him. As couriers go, he was a little short of the international class.

"Who gave you this?" I showed him the envelope.

He heaved his shoulder.

"Some guy down on the street. He gimme five to bring that up here. When I get back to him, there's another five."

So, by following the boy outside, I'd get a glimpse of the contact man. Which would tell me nothing, and upset the guy into the bargain.

"Go tell him there's no answer," I instructed.

Behind me, Florence sniffed her disapproval. The door closed behind the messenger, and I went back into my own room.

"Miss Digby, do you ever read the financial columns?"

"You know I don't."

"Then I recommend them to you. Also the labor news. We are living in hard times, Miss Digby, times of economic recession. This job pays five thousand dollars for three hours' work. That is almost seventeen hundred dollars per hour, not the kind of money a man can turn away. Besides, the approach intrigues me. I want to know who these people are, and why they picked on me."

"You'll probably all get to know one another quite well when you're in prison," she replied tartly.

"Here," I picked up the century notes and handed them to her, "go and deposit these. No, wait." I changed my mind and held one back. "For expenses."

She took the money and went away. Some people even manage to develop

4

a disapproving walk, and Florence is a star performer.

I sat at the window watching people moving reluctantly around in the afternoon heat. Even the traffic seemed to be crawling, and I was glad to be sitting in my nice cool office, with nothing to do but wait for the phone to ring.

It rang.

A man's voice, very guarded, said, "Mr. Preston? Mr. Mark Preston?"

"That's me," I confirmed.

I didn't bother to ask who he was, because he wasn't going to tell me anyway.

"You received an envelope a while ago?"

"I did."

"And you understood the message?"

"Not a word," I assured him. "I understood the five hundred bucks."

He thought about that for a few seconds.

"I see. But you intend to proceed?"

"I intend to go on listening."

Some people can be just as guarded as other people.

"You will be needed at eleven o'clock tonight. Drive to Wharf Ten. Park in Section D, Slot Number Twelve, and wait."

The docks. Could it be that Florence had been right, and this was some smuggling deal? No, I decided. All the details were wrong. Smugglers would not involve some complete outsider at the very last moment, the crucial moment.

"D 12?" I repeated. "Anything else?"

"No, that is all. Just sit in the car, and wait."

He hung up on me before I could think of any more questions. There were plenty of them, but they would have to wait, too. Like me.

The door opened, and La Digby came in.

"You won't go, of course?"

"Why won't I go of course? Hey, you were listening in on my private conversation."

"Well, of course I was," she snapped. "You'll probably need my evidence at the trial. I can testify that you didn't know what you were getting into, because I heard every word. What with me, and the doctor who will confirm that you are given to childish impulses, you'll probably get a light sentence. Well, are you going?"

I clicked my fingers at her.

"Affirmative. I have this childish impulse to get my hands on all that folding money. There are certain business interests in this town who will be glad to have me in a fluid cash position."

"Business interests?" she scoffed. "Certain bookmakers, you mean."

Until that moment I'd been in danger of forgetting that there were still three races to be run on the afternoon program out at Palmtrees. When she'd gone, in a disapproving huff, I ran my eye down the runners list. The five o'clock race included a short-price three-year-old named Wharf

7

Rat. If that wasn't an omen, I don't know what an omen is.

I telephoned Jule Keppler, and put my new hundred dollar note on the nose of this gift from the gods.

"Wharf Rat?" he repeated. "You got it."

I didn't have it for very long. Wharf Rat turned out to be one of those polite horses, the kind that thinks it's rude to push in front of people. There were six other runners in the race, and he politely let them all get in front of him, and stay there. To make things worse, the first one past the post rejoiced in the name of Dark Leaper.

If I'd known then what I know now, I'd have realised that was the real omen.

★ ★ ★

At ten-thirty that night I left the apartment and went down to the underground car park. The heat was still around, but I'd put on a light

8

sweater. Any breeze there is to be had in Monkton City of a summer's night concentrates along the coast. For extra added comfort, I'd tucked a well-worn thirty-eight Police Special inside my waistband. I didn't know what I was getting into, but I doubted if it was a Sunday School picnic. Unlocking the car door, I was about to climb in when I realised there was something on the seat. Pulling back, I looked quickly around, to see nothing but emptiness. Somebody had opened the car, left whatever it was, and then locked up behind them. Somebody who was now missing.

I decided there was no cause to fear the little parcel. If somebody had wanted to blow me up there are many much more certain ways to do it. No, this was a delivery, and I was the addressee. Nothing more. Intrigued, I pulled open the wrapper, and found myself clutching a wig. A blond wig, and a moustache to match. There was a note. It said:

Put these on. Important you not be identified.

To hell with that, I decided. I wasn't about to go parading around dressed up like some second-rate stick-up artist. Important, eh? Important to them, maybe, but they should have thought of that before they hired me. They should have looked around for somebody less well known. If they thought —

Wait a minute.

It could be that this was important to me, also. Maybe whatever I was going to deliver was of interest to other people, besides the ones who hired me. Maybe those other people would be interested in whatever was being carried, and the man who was carrying it. Maybe it wouldn't be such a dumb move for such people to be on the look-out for a fair-haired man with a moustache.

Reluctantly, I stuck the wig on my head, and peeked in the rear mirror. I looked like an extra from One Million

Years B.C. Then I realised the thing was supposed to be worn the other way around. That was better. In fact, that wasn't bad at all. The man looking back from the glass was not unlike me, but a few years older, more dignified. Encouraged, I put on the moustache, and found myself looking at a stranger. Not bad, I decided.

Not bad at all.

Getting into the spirit of the thing, I dug around the glove compartment for a pair of dark glasses, and that really completed the picture. This new man wasn't as attractive as me, naturally. He lacked a certain debonair quality, a panache, which I'm sure most people associated with me. He was more the kind of man you'd talk to about your retirement savings. Stable, if you know what I mean. And, if disguise was the name of the game, then I certainly had a good one.

Backing around, I drove slowly through the evening streets leading down to the dock area. There is something oddly forlorn about the wharves by night. During the day, the place is teeming with life and noise, people and machines engaged about their important affairs, an air of purpose everywhere. But once that six o'clock whistle blows, it's all over in a matter of minutes. What is left is row upon row of giant locked buildings, stark and featureless. An occasional chink of light from a watchman's office, where a sleeping geriatric is disturbed only by the two-hourly security checks of the roaming patrols. Huge grab cranes making grim outlines against the night sky, their steel jaws peering down in vain for something to clutch at. At the water's edge the sea laps darkly at the tethered vessels, cargoes and tramps mostly, which transport in and out the raw materials giving life to the coastline by day.

A dimly lit plate informed me reluctantly that I was about to enter Wharf Ten. The watch-office was unlit and unmanned, which meant the wharf was temporarily out of commission. I drove along to my allotted space at D 12 and pulled in, cutting the motor. There were a few trucks in view, no cars. It was then five minutes to eleven o'clock, and I sat watching the outside emptiness in the pale light of a fitful moon.

Precisely at eleven a car swung into view, and headed towards me. I patted at the thirty-eight, to remind myself it was still there. A man climbed out and walked towards me. I wound down the window as he bent over.

"Preston?"

It was the same voice I'd heard on the telephone.

"Right," I confirmed. "What happens now?"

Instead of answering, he straightened up and waved towards the car. The driver flashed his headlamps twice, and drove away.

My new friend said, "Let's go."

From the way he stood back from the door, he evidently meant we were going on foot. I got out and locked the door. He started to walk away, and I fell in beside him. He was of medium height, and very muscular beneath the heavy seaman's jersey. I couldn't make much of his face, since he wore one of those woollen hat things that cover the ears and half the cheeks.

"Where are we going?" I asked him.

He half-looked at me.

"Do you have a gun?" he demanded.

After a moment's hesitation, I nodded.

"Yes I do."

"Good."

He carried on walking towards the sea.

"Are we going swimming?" I demanded.

By way of reply he raised an arm, pointing. A small, powerful-looking cabin cruiser was rocking gently by the wharf-side.

"We're going for a little drive," he informed me tersely.

The night breeze clutched at my thin sweater and sneered. I was going to get frozen on that boat.

"I wish I'd been told," I grumbled. "I'd have put on something warmer."

"Don't worry. There'll be something on board you can borrow."

I could see a second man now, crouching at the stern of the boat. In his hands he cradled a short muzzled automatic rifle. He inspected me carefully as we drew close.

"This him?" he demanded.

"Yup."

"You have any trouble?"

"Didn't see a thing," replied my companion. Then to me, "You'll have to jump it. We didn't have time to rig up a gangway."

The man with the rifle chuckled.

"And try not to fall in," he counselled. "On account of the noise."

I waited until the deck was dipping towards me, then did my leaping act, landing on all fours. It wasn't very neat, but at least it wasn't wet. My escort did his own jump, and landed lightly on his feet.

"Let's go."

The guard handed him the rifle, and he settled down to watch the shore.

"C'm on."

I followed the second man into the wheelhouse, where he pointed to a locker.

"You'll find some stuff in there to keep you warm."

"Are we going far?" I asked him.

He looked pained.

"I just get paid to drive this thing, not to talk to the passengers."

He started the heavy engine, and we began to move away. Opening the locker, I found a thick sweater which looked about my size, and slipped it thankfully over my own clothes.

"O.K. to go outside?" I asked.

The helmsman shrugged.

"Help yourself."

I went out, to find the shore now well behind us. The first man was sitting on a pile of rope, the rifle beside him.

16

"Were you expecting trouble?" I queried.

"I always expect trouble," he informed me shortly. "Anyway, we can probably forget that now. Keep an eye open, though. There's always the coastguard."

I wondered why we needed to fear the defenders of our shores, but it would have been a waste of time to ask. On top of which, there was little chance of anyone spotting us, since we were not showing any lights.

Squatting down beside my escort, I fished out my pack of Old Favorites and tried to light up. After a dozen attempts I abandoned the idea, and threw the now-soggy tube away from me in disgust. It sailed back and hit me lightly on the chest. My companion chuckled.

"Not exactly Long John Silver, are you?"

"I've never been the same since the parrot died," I told him.

After that, I just stared out at the lightly swelling sea, feeling that immense loneliness brought on by limitless water. We must have been travelling for the greater part of thirty minutes, when quite suddenly all our lights were switched on. It was an unwelcome intrusion after the seclusion of the darkness.

"What's going on now?" I queried.

"We're outside the limit," was the laconic explanation. "You are now in international waters. Nobody can touch us here."

Great, I decided. The next piece of land, on the last map I ever looked at, would be somewhere like Hawaii. At this speed, we ought to make it in under two months. The man beside me had turned around to face forward, and now he nudged my arm.

"There she is."

And there she was. A sleek ocean-going yacht, all lights ablaze, riding the swell about half a mile ahead of us. Soon we were nosing in alongside a rope companion which had been lowered in readiness. Faces appeared at the rail above as the wheelman coaxed us gently into position.

"Up you go."

I didn't want to climb that swaying ladder. I wanted to stay in the nice safe cruiser.

"After you," I said politely.

"We're not coming. There's only you. Quit wasting time."

Gritting my teeth, I grabbed at my new enemy, and began the laborious climb. It seems to me there's too much fuss made about people climbing Everest and the like. Not enough attention is paid to private investigators risking life and limb out in the Pacific Ocean in the middle of the night.

Then there were hands, and strong muscular arms grabbing at me, and hauling me up and over the side.

"Up she comes," said a voice.

I was too thankful even to argue with him.

2

A COUPLE of sailors stood grinning at me.

"Boss is waiting to see you. C'm on," said one.

I walked along behind him, taking in the surroundings. I'd seen a few craft like it before. Playthings of multimillionaires, with every last refinement that money could buy, plus extra added sequins.

The sudden roar of an engine announced the departure of my recent companions, and I was alone out here in the middle of nowhere. The thought brought me little comfort.

We went through a sealed doorway into a passage that was all soft lights and deep carpet. There followed a maze of narrow turnings, until we reached an open space where a man sat in a deep club chair reading a magazine. He stood up, and the expensive suiting fell at once into faultless lines. His inspection of me was cool and impersonal. When he spoke, the thick East Coast accent did not match up to the suit.

"They tell me you're packing."

For a second I was surprised, then I realised my late escorts had been in radio touch with the ship.

"One thirty-eight," I agreed.

"Must be uncomfortable for you, toting that around. I'll kind of look after it, till you go."

He held out a hand, and after a moment's hesitation I lifted out the Police Special and handed it over. He grinned.

"Little old-fashioned, isn't it?"

"People I shoot it at don't seem to notice," I told him curtly.

"I guess. Wait here a minute."

He tapped at a door behind him, and went through. Then he emerged, crinkling fingers at me.

"In here."

I went through the door. A man

sat watching my entrance. He was short and totally round, inside a dressing-gown of rich brocade. The hooded black eyes, which stared at me unwinkingly, were set well back in a huge head. His face was hairless and smooth, and the top of the skull was heading in the same direction, except for a few remaining black hairs which had been tortured into a kind of flat kiss-curl in the centre of his forehead. The net effect was repulsive.

"Please close the door."

The words were carefully put together, making it obvious that he wasn't speaking his native tongue. I'd seen him somewhere before, or a picture of him.

"You may sit."

I sat, unable to take my eyes off him. He radiated power and strength, and authority. And something else. I wasn't certain what it was, but I didn't like it. He lifted a jewel-encrusted hand to his mouth and took a slow pull at a ten-inch cigar, still watching me.

"During our talk," he said, in that

slow precise diction, "I shall not use your name. This is not discourtesy, you must understand. It is for your own protection."

I did not understand at all.

"You mean this room might be bugged?" I queried.

He sighed.

"I do not know, but I trust no one. No one. Not even my own people, who have been with me for years. There are those who wish me harm. Those who would pay much money to accomplish this, and money, need I say, has strange effects on people."

That I understood, so I merely nodded.

It seemed to satisfy him.

"And so," he continued, "you will remain anonymous. It is possible that you may already have been seen by my enemies, perhaps even a photograph has been taken. I think you understand what I mean?"

Light flashed from many diamonds as he touched at his head. What he meant was, they could take all the pictures they liked of his fair-haired visitor with the bushy moustache. My own mother wouldn't have been able to identify me. This man was a planner, I realised. But it left me with a question.

"The men I first contacted," I asked, "the ones who brought me out here, you're trusting them."

The headshake was brief but dismissive. "No. Simple messengers. They were hired to bring you here, but they do not even know for whom they were working. They have been permitted to understand that they are involved in a high-class smuggling operation, which is something they can appreciate. They are not concerned with the details. There is one great advantage of hiring the criminal classes. They have this pathetic obsession with secrecy, even when it serves no purpose. Have you remembered yet?"

The question was delivered in the same precise monotone, and it took me by surprise.

"Remembered what?"

"You have been trying to recall why my face is so familiar."

The devil of it was, he was perfectly right.

"Yes," I admitted. "I'm sure I've seen you somewhere."

"I never seek publicity," he continued, "but it has lately been thrust upon me by enemies. I am Stavros Kurti. According to your Press, I am the eighth richest man in the world."

He paused then, to let me put the rest of it together. I was wishing I'd paid more attention to the story when it had broken a few weeks earlier. Kurti was being blamed as the key figure behind some huge international shipping swindle. There were half a dozen countries waiting for him with warrants, and the U.S. of A. was high up on the list. It helped to explain why he stayed outside the shore-limits. But it didn't explain what I was doing there, and I had a sneaking feeling I was out of my depth.

"I didn't read up on the case very closely," I admitted. "This financial scene is a little out of my line. I'm more into blackmail and murder, and minor infringements of that kind."

If he'd ever learned to smile, there would have been lines either side of his nose. The flesh remained impassively smooth.

"I am the victim of a conspiracy," he announced. "It will be resolved, naturally, and to my satisfaction. The finest lawyers and accountants in the world are hard at work on the matter at this very moment. The whole affair is an inconvenience, but no more. However, it is costing me a great deal of money, and this is a situation I cannot permit. Your government is holding ten of my ships idle whilst all this legal foolishness is in process. It must be stopped, and fortunately I am in a position to stop it. This is where I need your services."

Now we were through the bread, and getting to the filling. I put on my look

26

of serious concentration, and he noted it with approval.

"I have here a briefcase," and he pointed to the floor beside him. "In it, there is material vital to my application for the release of my ships from your shores. You are to deliver it."

I tried hard to keep scepticism out of my tone.

"There must be easier ways," I objected. "What ever happened to the good old United States mail service?"

He had been expecting something of the kind, and was ready for it.

"Your faith in such matters speaks well for your character," he informed me. "Regrettably, it does not reflect very creditably on your judgement. Your excellent mail service is a government agency, and no doubt beyond reproach. Unfortunately there are other official organisations without the same high reputation for integrity. I do not intend to be specific, but your own newspapers have uncovered some very disquieting situations in the past few years. It would be naïve to imagine that all these people operate within the rules. There are no rules. They are out to get me, and would regard the methods as unimportant. Such methods would undoubtedly include the suppression of the evidence in my support which is in this case."

I thought about that. It seemed to me he was chasing rainbows. Besides, I was taught not to believe everything I read in the papers. Still, if he wanted to imagine every shadow was hiding some kind of secret policeman, that was his business. Left to myself, I would have stuck a few stamps on the briefcase and dropped it in the nearest mail-box. If he preferred to hand over five thousand dollars for a personal delivery, I wasn't going to argue with him.

"O.K., Mr. Kurti, it's your money," I shrugged. "Where do I take the case?"

"It is not quite that simple," he demurred. "Let me first explain to you about the device."

Device? What did he mean, device?

Reaching down, he hauled up a flat metal briefcase covered in black plastic. It was the kind of thing catching on among people who wanted to be thought of as executive types, and would do no harm to the packet of sandwiches it normally carried.

"This is the case," he explained unnecessarily. "It is quite unremarkable in its appearance, as you see, the kind you can purchase almost anywhere. However, it has been modified. It can only be opened in a certain way, and I do not propose to enlighten you about that. Anyone who is not aware of the method of opening will set off an acid bomb. This will destroy the contents entirely. It will also, I regret, cause considerable physical harm to the person concerned."

Like burning off their hands, or worse. My lips were suddenly dry.

"And you expect me to carry that thing?"

He eyed me calmly.

CITY LIBRARY CORK

"It is perfectly harmless, I assure you. It cannot be activated accidentally. Only a positive attempt to open the case will trigger the mechanism. In other words, it will not harm anyone who wishes no harm to me."

I didn't like it. The idea of walking around with what amounted to a ticking bomb under my arm did not, as they say, appeal. But you had to give Kurti credit. His timing was like that of a magician. Before I could voice any more objections, he placed an envelope on the table. The flap was open, and the corners of a thick wad of one hundred dollar bills had been teased into a fan shape.

"There is five thousand dollars here. That was the amount quoted to you."

There's nothing will take a man's attention away from other things quite so fast as a wad of new currency notes. They looked good. Besides, where was the catch? The man had made it quite clear that the case wouldn't hurt anybody who had any right to open it. And anyway, it wouldn't arise. He would tell me where to take it. I would hand it over to the proper people, and that would be the end of it. You couldn't blame the man for wanting to take one or two little precautions.

On top of that, if he was willing to pay all that money, he wasn't going to take any chances with his precious evidence, whatever it was. No. I was letting my imagination run away with me again. Have to watch for that. It's the kind of luxury a man in my line can't afford. Especially if it's liable to cost him five big ones.

"All right, Mr. Kurti, you sold me. What happens now?"

There was no sign of triumph either on his face or his voice. He expected to win. Winning was the natural order of things.

"You will return to the mainland. By helicopter," he explained. "You will land at a spot I have selected in desert country, a few miles beyond your Monkton City. From there, you will proceed back to your apartment. You have a question?"

It must have been the way my mouth kept opening that gave him the lead.

"Just a small one," I admitted. "You are going to dump me and this — this parcel out in the wild blue yonder at one o'clock in the morning. How am I supposed to get home?"

"Why, your car will be waiting, naturally."

He seemed surprised that I should ask, and the more I thought about it, so did I. The fact that the keys to the car were in my pocket would present no problem to these people. After all, they managed to leave the wig inside without difficulty.

"Thank you. So I go back to the apartment. What happens then?"

"You retire for the night. Some time tomorrow you will receive a telephone call from a man named Ramondez. He will advise you as to the next step."

Ramondez. The name meant nothing.

"This call," I asked, "will it be

coming into the apartment, or to my office?"

"I cannot say," he hedged. "You will simply carry on as normal, but you will keep the briefcase with you at all times."

I didn't want it with me at all times. I wanted to be rid of it, and the sooner the better.

"But the call will be tomorrow, sometime?" I pressed.

"If all goes according to plan, yes." He looked at his watch. "The machine is ready now. I will not detain you."

He pushed the black bag towards me, and I stood up.

"I must be able to contact somebody," I told him.

He didn't understand at first.

"Whom did you wish to contact?"

"No, let's start again. I must ask you for an address, a telephone number, something. Don't forget, you're the one who says a lot of people would like to know about this little trip of mine. Suppose they catch up with me?

Suppose I get robbed? There has to be someone I can report to. What about this man Ramondez?"

The thick bulbous lips protruded even further while he considered. Or pretended to. Finally he nodded, opened a drawer, and took out a piece of paper which he slid across the desk. On it was written a telephone number. He'd had it in mind from the outset to give me the number. Otherwise, why would he have had it ready?

"If there is anything of serious importance, and I stress the word 'serious', then you may call this number between two o'clock and three o'clock, or six o'clock and seven. Two to three," he repeated, "or six to seven. There will be no one available at any other time to answer you. I trust that is clear?"

I pushed the note into a pocket.

"Quite clear. Er — " I gestured towards the money.

"Of course," he nodded. "Please accept your fee, and I wish you good fortune. When all these legal quibbles are ended, I shall be able to resume my operations in your splendid country. When I do, I shall not forget those who helped to make it possible. You may well hear from me again at that time."

If I'd been able to see into the future, my nod would have been less enthusiastic. Clutching gingerly at the briefcase, I made for the door. My temporary employer made no move to get up or even wave a hand. He simply watched me go, as he'd watched me enter.

Outside, the sentry stood up, holding out my thirty-eight.

"I'll show you the way."

There were more corridors, more turns and twists, until finally he leaned on a heavy metal lever, and we were out in the open again, but this time on a lower deck towards the bow. A civilian version of a military chopper squatted on the wooden planking. My escort touched me on the shoulder, pointing.

"There you go," he said.

A few members of the crew eyed me as I walked towards the waiting machine. Kurti's words were still fresh in my mind. Any one of these men could be noting down a careful mental description of the boss's visitor, for transmission to who-knew-what kind of forces back on shore. I was glad of the protection of all the fair whiskers I was sprouting. When I reached the helicopter, the pilot was already in his seat.

"Hi," he greeted. "Take the seat behind me, will you?"

I wasn't too pleased. The rear seat was not much more than a squashed bucket. There was a lot more room beside the driver, and the view would have been better, too. Well, he was the captain. I wedged myself into the narrow space, taking comfort from the fact that the journey would only be short.

There was the high-pitched whirr of a starter button, and the blades above began to slow revolve, which quickly picked up. The noise and vibration made an uncomfortable combination, and I inspected my upthrust knees without enthusiasm, waiting for him to slide the doors.

Suddenly, a head appeared at the passenger side. In the poor light, and with the face surrounded by a fur helmet, I could only just assess that the figure climbing in to the front was a woman. I forgot about my discomforts with the advent of this new travelling companion, and tried hard to get a good look at her. If she'd shown the same amount of interest in me, it would have been easier, but she faced resolutely to the front. The best view I could manage was of a good straight nose and high cheek-bones on an unlined face.

Now we were lifting off and up. I watched the good ship whatever-it-was shrinking away beneath us, then our nose turned inland, and there was nothing but sky and water. In what seemed like no time at all, the scattered lights of the night coastline appeared, and we were flying over good solid land. The pilot began to study the ground below, and finally tapped the woman on the shoulder, pointing downwards. She looked and nodded. He banked the little chopper, to enable him to make a final check lower down. Then, satisfied, he lowered us towards the desert floor, and stopped. I stared through the whirling dust to where two automobiles sat waiting. One was my own, the other a dark-coloured Cadillac, from which powerful headlamps now sprang to life as the car moved towards us.

The woman slid back the door beside her, and climbed out. She didn't even look at the pilot. I made to follow her, but a strong arm was thrust in front of me.

"Just hang on, mister. I'll tell you when," he shouted.

I huddled back in my bucket, and watched. The woman walked with an easy swinging stride towards the waiting Caddy. The driver leaped out and opened the rear door for her. The guy even touched his cap as she got in. Then he closed the door, hopped in the front and drove away.

It was two or three minutes before the restraining arm was removed.

"O.K."

I did my pushing and squeezing act again to get out. The Cadillac had made good use of the time and was nowhere in view.

"Thanks," I called. "Who was that lady?"

The pilot looked at me pityingly, shaking his head.

"Better get well clear," he replied. "I'm lifting off right away."

I had no wish to be choked to death by the dust under those chopping blades, so I ran rather than walked away. There was a roar as he increased the throttle, and then he was gone.

Suddenly, I was all alone. The desert air was cold, and there was an eerie sense of isolation. Just a few miles away was a fairly large city, with everything that entails. But here, in this dead spot in the middle of the night, I was just as much alone as the earliest pioneer or Indian, and I didn't like it. Wispy clouds floated across the watery moon, making sinister moving shadows from every rock, every clump of thirsty scrub. But I had something going for me which gave me the edge over those early travellers.

I had a comfortable solid automobile waiting, with plenty of gas in the tank. Holding tight onto the briefcase, I ran across to the welcoming car, unlocked the door and climbed in.

Soon, I was bowling along a dusty track, knowing roughly where the highway lay. Then, there it was, a broad metal ribbon that had never looked more becoming. There was little traffic around, and I kept my foot down all the way into town.

There was no one in my parking-slot at Parkside this time, and I turned tiredly into it and switched off the motor.

"Phew," I said, and began to open the door.

Something slammed viciously against the side of my head, and I flung up an arm against the darkness that rushed at me. There was a second hard blow, and after that I seemed to be falling, falling.

Just falling.

3

THERE was a pleasant, familiar smell under my nose. A comforting, evocative kind of smell, and I was trying to bring it to mind. Then I had it. It was leather, soft, yielding leather.

Leather?

But I don't have any leather on my bed. Neither does anybody else that I know of. Then what — I opened one eye and pulled my head upright. Pain jarred at the base of my skull, and a wave of nausea came over me. Something hard was pressing against my left side. Obviously a more methodical approach was needed. My half-open eye was an inch or so clear of what seemed to be the leather I'd been smelling. Good. Now, where do we find leather? The most likely answer seemed to be a car-seat. Fine. That would suggest that I was lying face down on the seat of a car, and therefore the hardness against my left hip would be the steering column. Very good indeed. The methodical approach will always produce results. They don't call me a big important detective for nothing.

The rest of it came quickly after that. Somebody had batted me over the head when I tried to get out of the car, and I had lost consciousness. The briefcase. Struggling upright, I ignored the searing pain behind my eyeballs, and searched frantically around. The daylight was strong, so I had been unconscious for several hours. This, and many other realisations, jumbled together in my mind as I scrabbled about looking for the precious case.

It was gone.

From the floor of the car I retrieved my Old Favorites, one handkerchief and a piece of paper with what looked like a telephone number. Someone had pulled my pants pockets inside out, to see what I was carrying. Another piece of memory clicked into place, and I yanked up my seaman jersey to feel inside my waistband. It was very comforting to feel the thirty-eight resting undisturbed, and behind it the envelope with the money Kurti had paid me for the little errand I was to do.

Was to have done, I corrected, as the full realisation of my new position finally came together and dropped with a hollow thud to the pit of my stomach. I was in a lot of trouble. Stavros Kurti was a man who paid for results, and he had paid me well for a simple enough job. I had goofed. It would be of no avail to say to a man like Kurti that I hadn't been expecting to get banged on the head. I should have been expecting trouble from the minute I left the ship. This was trouble merchandise I was carrying, and the reason I got paid so much money was because I was able to look after myself and the merchandise both. Or so it was assumed. Kurti wasn't sending an

44

apple for the teacher. He'd have given that to his four-year-old granddaughter, and asked her to be sure not to drop it. He was sending valuable property in care of someone who could be trusted to look after it. I was the someone, and I'd blown it.

Great.

After a final, pointless look around I clambered stiffly from the car and closed the door. My head banged with every movement, and I could feel a couple of very promising lumps where my assailant had given it to me good. Not wanting to scare the passers-by, I took a look at my appearance in a wing-mirror. A stranger stared back at me, and I realised the wig and moustache were still in position. About to yank them off, I changed my mind, without knowing quite why. Then I walked slowly across to the elevator and took myself up to the apartment. When I opened the door, it was with my left hand, my right being busy holding the automatic ready for visitors.

There was no one there, and no sign of disturbance. And why would there be? They had what they wanted. If you want to rob a dumb, over-confident character like me, there's no need to go to a lot of inconvenience, like burglarising the apartment. All you have to do is to hang around the garage and wait for me to produce the valuables.

What I wanted at that moment was to go to sleep for about three days, but sleep was out. It was almost seven o'clock in the morning, and that meant the people with the briefcase had four or five hours' start on me as it was. I wished I'd paid more attention to the time during the events of the night before, but I dismissed that as pointless thinking. In this kind of situation a start of ten minutes is long enough. When you talk in terms of hours, the exact number is irrelevant.

I put on some coffee, and tilted a measure of Scotch down my throat. It was fiery, and not very welcome down there, but it did infuse some kind of a glow. Stripping off, I stood under the shower, remembering just in time to remove my disguise. The thoughts came tumbling fast now, as the ice-cold needles drove against my protesting skin.

The important question was the identity of my attacker. It had to be someone who wanted the briefcase. Therefore, it had to be someone who could connect the briefcase with me. No, that didn't necessarily follow. It could also be someone who was looking for a man with fair hair and a moustache, without knowing I was underneath them.

So, where did that get me? As Preston, there were three possibles. One was the man who telephoned the office. The other two, assuming one of them did not make the call, were the characters who drove me out to Kurti's yacht. That took care of Preston.

The man in the wig was seen by the chopper pilot and the woman passenger. The pilot had taken off at once, so that ruled him out. The woman could have done it, but the method made no sense. Out in the desert would have been much more practical. There was at least one man with her there, the chauffeur, and maybe others inside the car for all I knew. No, for the moment I would discount the woman.

I concentrated instead on the two men in the power-boat. One of them knew me as Preston, the one who'd presumably left the disguise inside my car. The helmsman had stayed with the boat, and to the best of my recollection had not addressed me by name. These two had then driven my car out to the drop-point, and there certainly had to be two men on that job. One to deposit my car, and the second man in another car to lift him back to town. They couldn't just wait there for me, because the sight of a second car would have made me suspicious, and they knew I was armed. No, they had driven back to Monkton City and waited for me.

They knew where to wait, which confirmed my thoughts about the first man having been the one to leave the disguise in the first place. Yes, it had to be them.

So where did that get me? They were just two faces to me. I would know them again, naturally, but they would make certain I didn't get the opportunity. The boat. I suddenly remembered the boat. My late companions might disappear from view, but they couldn't pull the same trick with the boat. It was made of wood and steel and other excellent non-vanishing materials. I suddenly felt very affectionate towards the boat. It could be traced.

The man who could help me was Matt Newman. Matt is an old friend, who earns his living by taking out parties of well-to-do fishermen, or running summer visitors out to Catalina for the day. Anything which turns a dollar, so long as it's connected with the sea. Picking up the phone, I dialled his number, hoping he hadn't already set off on an early trip.

He answered at once, with a growled 'Hallo'.

"Matt? Mark Preston. How are you?"

"Preston?" he queried. "At this hour?"

"I couldn't sleep," I replied. "Listen, are you working today?"

"Got a late start," he informed me. "Bunch of big sportsmen who won't leave before nine o'clock. Well, it's their money. What's up?"

"I'm trying to trace a boat," I told him. "Thought you might be able to help me."

"Maybe," he said, non-committally. "What's the make and class?"

"I don't know," I admitted. "I could describe her to you — "

"Ha-ha. I bet you could. It was sharp at the front and kind of rounded off at the back, right? That might help us."

When he put it like that, I realised the telephone conversation was not going to produce results. Matt was quite right. Any description I came up with would not exactly classify as expert testimony.

"Maybe if I came down there I could do better?" I suggested.

"You'd need to hurry. At nine sharp I have to go scare off the fish."

We broke the connection, and I started to pull on some clothes. On the floor, in a crumpled heap, lay the big jersey I'd been loaned the night before. Might as well look the part, I decided, picking it up. Straightening it out, I realised I was about to don it back to front, so I flipped it over. Then I froze in my bending position.

Stencilled on the back in clear white lettering was a legend — s.s. *Monkton Pride*.

So now I knew the name of the boat. That would shorten my visit to Matt Newman. Now that I had the name, all I needed to know was how to check on the registration and so forth. I was feeling better already, and decided against wearing the jersey after all. Other people can read just as well as me, and I didn't want to attract unwelcome attention. Bundling my precious clue under one arm, I set out to keep my appointment.

Newman and his ilk occupy a section of the beach entirely different from the dock area I'd visited the previous night. That was the functional side of the sea, the wharf, crane and warehouse aspect. A mile south, the aspect changes considerably, and for the better. Sandy beaches, littered with all kinds of pleasure-craft, and peopled with those special characters who can't thrive away from that deep blue water. Endlessly polishing, painting, or just scrubbing decks. Busy at a hundred and one tasks, which never seem to have an end. It's a community of its own, a place of chandlers' huts, fresh crab and beer joints, and an overall air of genial camaraderie, far removed from the harsher realities of the outside world.

Newman was sitting on top of the wheelhouse of his immaculate power-boat, legs dangling over the side, and watching me negotiate the narrow plank which led aboard.

"Hi," he greeted. "What's all this about?"

Matt must be about forty years old, but only in the tanned and weather-seamed face. The rest of him is twenty, all lean, packed muscle and agility.

"Hallo, Matt, mind if we go inside?"

"Kay."

He leaped nimbly down on bare feet and opened a door, waving me in.

"I get the impression this is confidential?" he queried.

The light blue piercing eyes searched my face for signs of evasion. I didn't want to involve an old friend in whatever trouble was to come, so I had my story ready.

"There's a thing I'm working on," I told him. "Last night, it led me to follow a couple of characters who may be able to help. They went down to the docks, jumped aboard this kind of cabin cruiser, and took off. It's important that I should find them. If they spotted me, they could have gone to ground. But they can't hide the boat."

He listened, with pursed lips.

"I see. Well, I don't know whether I can help, but I can try. Let's have a description."

I pulled open the jersey.

"I can do better," I said proudly. "I know the name. One of them dropped this while he was running. The boat is called the s.s. *Monkton Pride*."

His hand had been held out to take the jersey from me. Now, he dropped it and stared at me blankly.

"The *Monkton Pride*?" he repeated incredulously.

"Sure. It says so right here. Look."

I unrolled the heavy wool, and he stared at it, shaking his head from side to side.

"You know my rule," he said, "no drinking before the sun is high. I'm going to break it. You want a beer?"

Without waiting for an answer he opened a refrigerated cupboard and lifted out two cans, passing one to me. Ripping open his own, he drank from it, and then sat down.

"This thing you said you were working on," he said, almost as if to himself. "Care to tell me anything about it?"

I hesitated.

"Tell you the truth, Matt, I don't especially want to," I replied slowly. "I'll just tell you it's big, and it could be dangerous. I certainly don't want to get my friends mixed up in it."

"H'm. And you say you picked that up after some guy dropped it? Running away from you, as I understand it."

"That's right," I confirmed. "Why?"

"Why? Let me tell you. Because that little item you're holding is supposed to be keeping fish warm, one hundred fathoms down, off the Azores."

I sat down then, and stared across at him.

"I'm not following you, Matt. Listen, I saw this boat only last night."

"No," he interrupted. "You saw a boat, this kind of boat. The *Monkton Pride* was a ten thousand tonner."

"Perhaps you'd better tell me about it," I suggested.

He pushed the ice-cold can around between his fingers.

"It was all in the papers. No secret. Of course, there was plenty of beach-rat chatter, but there always is. You really don't remember, do you?"

"Maybe it'll all come back. Try me."

"The *Pride* operated under one of these Liberian flags. You know the dodge? A couple of people set up a company with a Liberian registration. It's a device for evading all kinds of legalities, especially safety regulations."

"I think I've heard something about that," I admitted.

"Right. Well the *Pride* went down,

56

under very strange circumstances — it must be three months ago now. There was one hell of a fuss, because the insurance runs into millions."

"I see. Are you saying the crew went down, too?"

"No. I don't think there were any casualties. But they were all Asiatics and the like. There were no American seamen on board, except the captain and engineer, and they wouldn't have been wearing that."

He jabbed a finger towards my prized jersey.

"Why not?"

"That's working gear," he explained. "That belongs to a seaman."

Now that I had the story, I thought I detected a flaw in his reasoning.

"But the ship's presumably been around for years?" I queried. "There could be plenty of people around who served on her at one time or another. They could well have forgotten to return a jersey. Half those people out there right now are probably wearing stuff that started life on some other ship."

He didn't seem overly impressed.

"Could be," he said grudgingly. "Only thing is, the guy who dropped that is no sailor. Not a real one. Sea-going people are very superstitious. You won't find them wearing things with the name of ships that are in the big deep. They might keep such things at home, like souvenirs, but wear them? No."

I thought he was making too much of it, but I didn't want to offend him. There was another thing, too. Matt Newman had set off a whole new train of thought in my mind, which may or may not be productive. If it should be, then there was all the more reason to keep him out of it.

"Well, Matt, that's a fascinating story, but the thing I'm doing is not in that big international class. I just want a word with these two comics who got away last night. Could we get back to the real boat, the one I actually saw?"

He was evidently reluctant to leave such a dramatic topic, but he shrugged in resignation.

"Tell me about the boat."

I gave him the best description I could, and then the questions began. Listening to experts always gives me a lift, and Newman was an expert. His questions were mostly eliminators, and it was like a policeman trying to put together a photo-fit. After about fifteen minutes of this, he nodded.

"I think we might be getting somewhere. Let's try some pictures."

Crossing to a bookshelf, he thumbed his way along, finally selecting a thick volume and turning the pages as he came back to his seat. He held out a page for me to inspect. There were four entries to the page, each with a black and white photograph, and a set of specifications alongside.

"How do you like that one?"

He pointed to the third picture down. It certainly looked very like the boat I'd travelled on the previous night, but there was something not quite right about it.

"I don't know," I said doubtfully. "It's very like it, but I would have had to jump aboard about there, and — " and I stabbed with a finger " — on this one I'd have tripped over that rail."

"Good. We're getting warm then. Try this one."

He turned more pages, and offered another photograph. It was closer, but there was still something not quite right. I wished I'd been paying more attention, and I said so.

"You're doing very well," he consoled. "We have to be getting close now."

We tried two more pictures, and I was beginning to think we'd never come up with the answer.

"These are so very close, Matt, maybe I'm getting punchy."

He rubbed at his chin.

"There's a class very like these that I haven't shown you. And for a good reason. There's a man over in Cape Cod who produced his own version of this class, but she would have to be a long way from home. Maybe it's worth a try."

Returning the book to its place on the shelf, he selected another, and stood rifling at the pages.

"What do you think of this?"

He put another picture in front of me. All it lacked was a man squatting in the stern with a rifle on his knee. I sighed with relief.

"That's it, Matt. I mean, it isn't merely like it. That is the actual boat I saw."

"H'm." He sat down, staring at the picture, and then at me. "And you're absolutely sure?"

"I'm sure."

"Well, it shouldn't be hard to find. Tell you the truth, Mark, I'm getting kind of excited about this myself. Like me to help you track her down? I could cut a lot of corners with people like the harbour master. Don't forget these are my waters you're splashing around in."

As offers go, it was tempting. He could probably save me a lot of time, plus unwelcome attention. It's one thing for one of the crowd to ask questions, it's quite another for an outsider to come poking around. And I was very much the outsider.

"Well," I hedged, "there's no doubt I could use the help. But I have to be honest with you, Matt. This could turn out to be more than it seems. These guys can play a rough game."

"Oh pshaw. You wouldn't let the nasty bogeyman hurt me, would you?"

His eyes twinkled, and I recalled the last time a couple of bogey men had set out with that intention. They were probably still paying off the hospital bills.

"I'd be glad of the help," I admitted.

4

ONE hour later I stood on the beach, waving off Matt Newman and his party of overweight sportsmen. His main concern, as he privately admitted, was not with how many fish they brought back. He was far more worried about returning with the same number of fishermen as he started out with.

He'd been right about the value of his contribution. In the space of a dozen telephone calls he had been able to track down the boat I was seeking. These shore-based mariners operate a kind of secret society of their own, and it might have taken me days to come up with the kind of help Matt Newman could call on simply by dialling a number. The proper description of my quarry turned out to be motor-launch, and the name was *Eskay Three*. Nobody seemed to know what became of *Eskay One* and *Two*, and certainly no one could offer any clue as to what the significance of Eskay was. The best suggestion put forward was that the word was a contraction for Eskimo Kayak, and that some eskimo who'd struck it rich was having his little joke on the yachting world. I had reservations about this solution, but I kept them to myself. It struck me as altogether too great a coincidence that I should be taken out to see Stavros Kurti in a launch called *Eskay Three*, or, as you might care to write it down, *S.K. Three*. It was no part of my plan to draw attention to any connection between the shipping magnate and myself.

Matt had learned that the launch was harboured and maintained by a local firm of ships' engineers called Seasport Limited. They had their moorings a short drive from Matt's own, and I now headed down there, after watching him disappear from view.

Seasport was no ramshackle, one-man operation. It was a row of smartly painted boat-housings, and every appearance of the millionaire service on offer. This was no place to hire a dinghy for a day on the lake, as the row of gleaming limos in the park testified. I left the car at a respectful distance from its betters and followed the signs marked 'Office'.

Inside, a heavy man sat behind a desk, sweating in the early heat, and in deep discussion with another man standing in front of him. The second man was tall and slim, in a well-cut lightweight suit of pale gray, and the clean-shaven face turned at my entrance was not friendly.

"Oh, I didn't want to interrupt," I said. "I'll wait outside."

I turned to go, but the heavy man called after me.

"Wait a minute, this could take some time. Is your business quick?"

"I hope so," I replied. "Just want to trace one of your motor-launches."

"Shouldn't take long. Our records are always up to date," he assured me. "Which one are you interested in?"

"The *Eskay Three*," I told him.

The second man had been staring at his feet and looking bored. Now, he looked sharply at me, and he wasn't bored at all.

"*Eskay Three*?" he said quickly. "What do you want her for?"

I hesitated, weighing up the situation. Until now I'd just been a man horning in on a conversation. Now, I was the focus of all attention. Maybe I'd gone about this all wrong, but it was too late in the day for that kind of thinking.

To the lightweight suit I said, "This man here," pointing behind the desk, "seems to be some sort of company official. I don't mind him asking me questions. But just who are you, exactly?"

"I'm Inspector Cutter of Dock Security," he replied evenly. "That's just who I am. Exactly. Now, who are you, and what do you want with the launch?"

"Name is Preston," I told him. "I met a couple of guys in a bar last night. They said we could go out fishing today if I could put up fifty for my share of the gas. Not against the law, is it?"

The company man sighed.

"You'll get no fishing on that craft today. Better go home and forget it, Mr. Preston."

I shrugged and made to leave.

"No, wait."

Inspector Cutter hadn't finished with me. I'd been afraid of that. Now I turned and waited.

The inspector walked around as though deep in thought. When he next spoke he had somehow got between me and the door.

"These two men," he queried. "Tell me about them."

"Just men," I said innocently. "What is there to tell?"

He nodded, as though I'd said

something intelligent.

"What were their names, for one thing?"

"I don't know," I denied. "I didn't ask. Tell you the truth, even if they'd told me I might not have remembered. Had one or two drinks, know what I mean?"

He smiled. I tried to recall where I'd seen a thinner smile, but it came up zero.

"Sure I understand. But you managed to recall the name of the launch, and the name of this company too. Now that's strange, wouldn't you say?"

But this time I had something going for me.

"Not too strange," I contradicted. "Considering I had it written down."

I had, too. Matt Newman had repeated the information given to him over the telephone, and I had noted it carefully as he did so. Inspector Cutter held out a hand.

"Mind if I see?"

"No, certainly not."

I fished in my pocket for the scribbled note, and held it out for him to see. He inspected it carefully, trying to find something wrong with it. The heavy man had craned over the desk to look for himself. Now he settled noisily back, and waited for the security man's next move. So did I.

"All right," said Cutter wearily. "So you wrote down these things and forgot the names of the men. What did they look like? You can remember that, can't you?"

But I'd had time to put myself together now, and that piece of action with the note had restored my confidence.

"Look," I said reasonably. "I'm just a man who came down here for the fishing. I don't have to answer any of your questions unless I feel like it. I'm not an unreasonable man, but if you want any co-operation from me, you'd better start by telling me what this is all about."

"You think so, eh?"

He was beginning not to like me, and it was mutual.

"I think so," I confirmed.

"Do you know that Dock Security has powers of arrest?" he demanded.

I did. I also knew that those powers ceased at the boundary of the docks, but I didn't want to antagonise him too much. Neither did I want to seem too much of an expert in such matters. It doesn't always pay dividends.

"Well, I imagine so," I returned. "I'd never thought about it."

"Think about it," he advised. "It might make you a little more co-operative."

I feigned exasperation.

"Look, I don't mind co-operating. But I have to know what it is I'm co-operating about. That's not unreasonable, is it?"

The heavy man sighed and looked out the window. I had a feeling he was on my side. There was a metal plate in front of the desk, reading 'J. Haines'. When he spoke, his tone was soft and placatory, but his meaning was clear.

"C'm on, Ed, why don't you tell the man what's going on? You can't come all this J. Edgar Hoover when you're outside your jurisdiction."

Cutter clicked his tongue in annoyance. Haines had cut the ground from under his feet.

"All right," he conceded. "What's going on is this. A man was found on the *Eskay Three* a few hours ago. He'd been shot to death, and that makes it murder. Now will you co-operate?"

I wished I hadn't asked.

"Tell you anything I can," I assured him. "Murder, huh? Did the other man do it?"

"That's police business," he snapped, meaning he didn't know. "Now, let's have those descriptions."

It wasn't easy to describe people I'd only seen in the half-light of the moon, and both wearing those woollen head-coverings, but I had a shot at it. He listened.

"Would you be able to identify these

men?" he demanded.

My look of doubt was not assumed.

"I could try, but you must remember I just met them the one time. I wouldn't want to think a man would go to the gas-chamber on my say-so. Was it one of my two who got killed?"

He didn't like to answer questions. He was in the asking business.

"Could be," he admitted reluctantly. "Your description of the man you called One could just about fit our corpse."

"So you'll be looking for the other guy," I said reflectively. "They seemed to be together all right, you know, like regular buddies. It doesn't sound right that a man could kill his buddy."

I'd said exactly the right thing. It was the kind of remark a citizen might well make, and it improved the atmosphere. It made me Joe Public, The Average Man, and it made Cutter the knowing professional. He even smiled.

"That just shows how little you know," he said smugly. "In this kind of situation it's always somebody close we want to talk to. You said yourself they'd been drinking, and that starts trouble as often as not. We'll need a statement, by the way. Where can we reach you?"

I gave him the Parkside address, and he whistled.

"With an address like that, you shouldn't ought to go boozing in waterfront bars. There's some very undesirable characters around those places."

It was statement and question in one, but I took it at its face value.

"You're right there. I'll have to be more careful where I drink."

Haines was watching my face, and I had the feeling I wasn't fooling him at all.

"You still want to go fishing?" he demanded. "Might be able to fix you up, although you've left it pretty late. We're about through, aren't we, Ed?"

Inspector Cutter hesitated. What Haines had said amounted to a dismissal. I was there on business, and if he lingered the company would have cause for complaint that he was interfering with the conduct of their affairs. And, he had little real authority.

"Well," he said finally, "I guess there isn't much more for me to do here. Thanks for all the help, Jack, and I'll probably be in touch again. Don't forget about that statement, Mr. Preston."

He hated calling me 'Mr.'

"Ready when you call me, inspector," I assured him.

One final nod and he went away. When the door was closed Haines relaxed back in his chair.

"You mustn't mind Ed," he advised me. "Fact is, this killing isn't going down too well in certain places. Seems that half the night security force was conking off, and Ed Cutter is going to have a lot of explaining to do."

I remembered the absence of security people when I kept my rendezvous at Wharf Ten the night before. I shrugged.

"Man has his work to do. I understand his position."

Haines nodded, staring at me shrewdly.

"Well, he's gone now. Suppose you tell me what this is all about?"

It took me by surprise.

"All about?" I repeated. "Why, these two guys — "

"No, no," he interrupted. "That was for Cutter. He isn't here now. I know you're a friend of Matt Newman's. He's been phoning everybody on the coast, trying to find the *Eskay Three*. He wouldn't do that for any fisherman. So?"

It wouldn't do me any good to wriggle. In any case, I owed this man. He'd kept quiet about Matt Newman while Inspector Cutter was in the office. Matt was of the fraternity, and the security man was not. They'd helped me once, and they might be able to help again, but not if they thought I wasn't playing square.

"I'm a private investigator," I told him, and produced my I.D.

He looked at it without comment, and waited.

"I'm working on an enquiry which leads off in all kinds of directions," I continued. "One of them brought me down here. Matt is an old friend, and I knew he'd help out if he could. I'm not really interested in the boat at all. It was these two men I wanted to talk with. Now, it looks as if I'll have to settle for one."

The blue stubble on his throat rasped as he ran a paw-like hand up and down.

"I don't want to seem inquisitive," he said blandly, "but it couldn't be that you already rubbed out one of these characters, and you want to find the other one for the same reason?"

I grinned. This Haines and I could get along.

"Not this trip," I denied. "You heard what Cutter said. The murder was done during the small hours. I never bump off anybody between midnight and six a.m. It's a house rule."

"H'm." He wasn't sure whether to believe me or not. What I had to rely on was his good opinion of Matt Newman. "Tell you the truth, this whole thing has me puzzled. That launch was in my care, and nobody told me these people had any authority to use it."

"You mean they just stole it?"

He shook his head.

"No, that's the strange part. There's a special set of keys for that craft. I mean, some of those out there you could start with a hairpin. But not the *Eskay Three*. There are three special keys that have to be used before you can even get access to the engine. If these two had just wanted to borrow a boat, there's a dozen out there wouldn't present any problem. But they took the one that couldn't be borrowed, and that means they had keys."

I thought about that for a moment,

then made a suggestion.

"How's this. They knew they'd only need the boat for a few hours. That way they'd have it back where it belonged before your people came to work today. Nobody need ever know it had been out. Does that makes sense?"

Haines reflected carefully, then gave a half-nod.

"It would, if they'd brought it back like you said. As it is — "

The massive shoulders heaved up and down.

"As it is," I persisted, "one of the men who intended to have it safely back here got himself murdered. He could scarcely have expected that, now could he? We don't know whether his partner killed him or not, but he must know something about it. Otherwise, where is he?"

"Yes. Yes, I see what you mean. Could be. Let's think about that. There's these two men, coming down here to use the boat during the night. We don't know what for, but we can assume it's something illegal, which is why I wasn't notified in the first place. Whatever it is they're doing, something goes adrift, and one of them gets himself killed. The other man either killed him, or flies into a panic and takes off. Either way, the *Eskay Three* does not get returned as planned. Yes, that all sounds possible. But where does it get us?"

He knew the answer to that as well as I did, but there was no way I could avoid bringing it up.

"Mr. Haines," I said, half-apologetically, "it gets us to wondering about the man who gave them the keys. Could it have been one of your staff?"

"No," he denied with assurance. "First thing I checked. There's only one set in my care, and they're right here in the desk."

"Then that only leaves the owner," I pointed out. "He must have given them the O.K. Does Inspector Cutter know about this?"

Haines' headshake was decisive.

"No. I have to protect my customers, and the good name of this company. If there are going to be any policemen banging on doors then my customer is entitled to whatever notice I can give."

"You wouldn't care to tell me how I can contact the owner?" I asked innocently.

He looked pained.

"Be your age. I don't mind helping out a friend of Matt's, but this is a customer we're talking about."

It was no more than I had expected. But I couldn't leave it there.

"This man who was killed," I pressed. "Did Cutter tell you his name?"

"No harm in that I can see," he replied. "Be in all the papers anyhow. Name of Street. Burton Street, I think he said. Meant nothing to me. How 'bout you?"

I shook my head.

"Nothing," I confirmed. "Do you have any idea who the missing partner might be?"

"Been thinking about that." He frowned in concentration. "You see, that launch needs handling. She isn't just any old coast-hugger. How can I explain it to you? Horses. That's it, horses."

My face must have encouraged him. He wasn't to know that here was a subject I could understand, and I have the betting-slips to prove it.

"Horses?"

"Yeah. An ordinary joe goes down to the riding stable. What he wants is to get up on something that looks like a horse, plod around for an hour or two. They have horses for people like that. They're quiet, reliable, harmless. The guy will make like John Wayne for a while, and he won't get hurt. Neither will the horse. The stable may have a couple of real thoroughbreds. Temperamental. Live wires, if you follow me. But they don't let the amateurs get near them. Boats are like that. Are you catching this?"

I was, and it made sense.

"So you're saying the owner wouldn't trust just anybody with the *Eskay Three*. It would have to be a real seaman, an expert."

"Right. All the time that launch has been with me, I've only known three people take her out."

This was getting better by the minute.

"You heard my description, when I was talking to Cutter. Does it sound like any of your three?"

"Only one fits," he told me. "The other guy is well over six feet tall and bony like a skeleton. Nothing like what you described."

"The other guy," I questioned. "I thought you said there were three men?"

"No," he denied. "I said three people. One of them is a woman, so she's out. It comes back to Angie, I think."

"Angie?"

"Angelo Castanna. Your description, you'll excuse me, it wasn't very good.

82

But of those I know who can be trusted with the *Eskay Three*, Angie is closest. Plus, he has a reputation for being impulsive, with his fists or a knife, or anything else that comes to hand. Be worth your while to give him some attention."

When he spoke of Castanna, it was without warmth.

"You don't like him too well."

Haines made a face.

"A real wharf-rat, the kind that gets us all a bad name. He'll turn his hand to anything, except work. But when it comes to boats, the guy is a whizz, a real engineers' engineer. If he was different from the way he is, he could be running his own outfit. That man really knows his boats. And the sea."

I was loving this. If somebody wanted a night-ride out into the middle of the ocean, one passenger to be delivered, and no questions asked, Angelo Castanna could have been home-crafted for the job.

"I suppose you wouldn't have any

idea where I could look for him?" I asked tentatively.

Haines smirked derisively.

"If he bumped off this what's-his-name, this Street, I imagine he's half-way to Baja California by this time. There's a thousand rat-holes along the coastline where a character like that can disappear."

"I appreciate that," I assured him, "but I was thinking more of wherever he lives when he's home. Maybe somebody around there could give me a hand."

"I wouldn't know," he told me. "There's a joint down the beach called the Hairy Crab. Guys like Castanna use it as a kind of club. You could ask there. But watch your back."

I shook hands with him. Haines had been a real help to me, and that was one more I owed Matt Newman.

"I'll let you know how it all comes out," I told him.

"Do that," he grinned.

When I got back to the car, I sat for a while, looking out at the dappled sea, and thinking. If Castanna was the killer, it was fair to assume that he now had the briefcase. I couldn't accept that there was any other reason for my two escorts to fall out. And so, if he had the case, he would not run off with it, whatever Haines might think. He would know it was valuable, even if he didn't know why. Either he would try to open it, in which case he'd get a nasty, possibly fatal shock, or, if he knew that was dangerous, he'd be offering his prize for sale.

Whichever way he decided to jump, he wasn't going to be hundreds of miles away. He was going to be right where the action was, and that meant somewhere in Monkton City.

It seemed like a good time to take refreshment in a place called the Hairy Crab.

5

THE average beach club is a pleasant place, with cool verandahs and the soothing sounds of tinkling ice in tall glasses. There are photographs of giant rays, and shipwrecks, pieces of tarred rope, ships' wheels, and other nautical bric-à-brac.

The proud owners of the Hairy Crab didn't believe in too much by way of such trappings. A crazy-hinged, wood-slatted door led into a dark and noisome room almost bare of furniture. To one side, a long greasy counter represented the bar, and it was in care of a huge mulatto in a grimy undershirt, with a shaven head and one gold ear-ring. There was one other customer at that early time of morning, and he paid me no attention whatever, probably because he was curled up on the floor with his back to me.

The mulatto stared at me with dislike.

"We don't wanta buy nothing," he rasped. "Blow."

"Oh tut," I tutted, "that's no way to talk to an old seafaring man. Not matey, at all."

He squinted along the side of a vast sprawling nose.

"Seafaring man?" he sneered. "What line might you be with? Matey."

Leaning on the counter, I beckoned him to bend down while I whispered.

"I'm just off the s.s. *Mint*," I told him.

"Mint? Never heard of it," he growled.

"Oh yes, really. We just shipped a whole lot of cargo in here. I brought some of it with me. Look."

I spread a ten-spot on the counter, where he could see it, but not reach it. He stared at it lovingly.

"Insurance joker?"

"Now, what makes you think that?" I asked, intrigued.

He managed to tear his eyes away from the bill.

"You're a stranger," he explained. "We only get three kinds. Cops we get. They come in strong, shouting around and waving their muscles. Tourists we get. They come in to get atmosphere, real seamen's atmosphere. They don't stay long. The third kind is your kind. Always waving that green stuff about. Insurance, right?"

I could follow his reasoning. I could also understand why the insurance men would home in on the Hairy Crab. If anything had gone missing, this was just the kind of place that could provide a lead.

"Kind of insurance," I admitted.

"I knew it. Well, we don't know nothing about it."

"I didn't ask any question yet," I pointed out.

Brown muscle rippled alarmingly from the broad shoulders and along bare arms that could have done duty as anchor-ropes.

"The question don't matter," he assured me. "Whatever it is, we don't know nothing about it."

I moved the ten to where he could reach. A hand like a side of bacon covered it instantly, and he grinned, like a wolf who just spotted a stray lamb.

"That pays for my time. Now blow."

"In a minute. Tell me where I can find Angelo Castanna."

He shook his head.

"Never heard of him."

I produced another ten, keeping it clear of the grab crane he was using as an arm.

"I got another one, see? Now then, tell me how to locate Castanna, and you can keep them both. Otherwise I'll take them both away."

He looked puzzled.

"I don't get it," he confessed. "I could break your back with one hand. What makes you talk so big?"

"This does."

Pulling out the thirty-eight, I held it in his general direction, and he backed off.

"What was that name again?"

"Castanna. Angelo."

"And I get the other ten?"

By way of answer I pushed it closer to him, but he didn't touch it.

"He has a room at Feeny's place."

"Where's that?"

"River Street."

Great. I was really mixing in society today. First the Hairy Crab, then some flea-bag on River Street.

"If you're telling me one of those seaman's yarns, I'll be back."

I went out carefully, not turning my back on him. Then I pointed the car inland, and went looking for Feeny's. The manager there didn't like me either, but he led me protestingly to a room on the second floor, which Castanna rented by the week. There was nobody home, and I had to spread another ten to get him to open the door. Surprisingly enough, the room was very neat. Everything was clean and tidy, and impersonal. There was no sign that the occupant had been intending to move on, not if his few belongings meant anything to him. The bed had not been slept in. I don't know what I'd been hoping to find in there, but there was nothing useful.

"You seen enough, mister?" demanded the manager. "I'm taking an awful chance letting you in here, you know."

I nodded.

"You have no idea where he might have gone?"

"Who says he went anywhere?" he countered. "His stuff is right here, you can see it for yourself."

That was true enough, and there was no point in my hanging around any longer.

"O.K.," I nodded, "you want to make another twenty-five?"

He whistled.

"Doesn't everybody? Who do you want killed?"

"All you have to do to earn it is make a phone call. And one more thing. Anybody else comes around here asking questions, you don't tell them about me, or the telephone number. Are we still talking?"

"You got it. Just call me Mr. Stumm."

"Here's the number to call." I scribbled out the number of the office. "If Castanna shows up, let me know at once. If there's anybody else after him, I want to know that, too. But I have to know exactly who's doing the asking, and anything else you can find out about them. You got that all straight?"

He repeated what I expected for my money, and I gave him five in advance. Then I went gladly downstairs, and out into the open air. The atmosphere on River Street is nothing to rave about, but it smelled like a morning in spring after the interior of Feeny's Hotel for Men.

I wasn't at all certain I could trust the

manager, but I had to start somewhere. Soon now, Stavros Kurti would be getting on my tail, looking for his precious briefcase. I wasn't looking forward to my conversation with his emissary, but at least I could say I hadn't been twiddling my thumbs.

When I got to the office, Florence Digby looked at me expectantly.

"Good morning," she greeted. "How did it go last night?"

It isn't that I don't trust Florence, but I make it a rule not to fill her head with extraneous information.

"Routine," I assured her.

She didn't believe me.

"H'm," she sniffed. "Well, if you won't tell me, you won't. Did it take all night? You look like the wreck of the *Hesperus*."

It's always a comfort to have a woman's soothing words. In any case, she had the wrong ship. She ought to have said the *Monkton Pride*.

"Nice to have your vote," I assured her. "See if you can get hold of Sam

Thompson, will you? I need him here on the run."

"I'll see if he's available," she returned primly.

Thompson, when available, is one of the best legmen in the business. The problem is, he doesn't work at it. What he works at is trying to drink the town dry, and he's good at that too, but it brings a problem with it. The stuff has to be paid for, preferably with money. To get money, people have to work. And so, as soon as the bartenders stop smiling and start threatening, Sam Thompson trudges back to the work force, and becomes available. Then, once he straightens out the finances, he'll go missing again, and the process repeats itself. In all the time I've known him he's never succeeded in striking a balance between these two major aspects of his life. Some day I'm going to write a thesis about this sociological peculiarity, and I shall call it the Thompson Dichotomy. Trouble is, I'm not really sure how to spell dichotomy.

There was nothing on my desk but the morning paper, and I searched quickly for any reference to the murder at the docks. There was nothing, so it must have occurred too late to make the edition.

The phone rang. I picked it up and said, "Preston."

A woman's voice said, "Is that Mr. Mark Preston?"

It sounded like oil being poured over velvet. I sat up a little straighter in the chair. A man doesn't want to look like a slob around a voice like that.

"That's me," I confirmed. "Who am I speaking to, please?"

"My name is Stella Raymond," she told me, and I rolled it round my tongue. "I'd like to talk to you, Mr. Preston. Could you possibly come to see me?"

She was kidding, really. Any man would follow that voice anywhere, and she must know it. Mentally, I was half-way to the door already, then I remembered the call from Kurti's man, and my spirits dropped.

"I'd be glad to, Mrs. Raymond," I assured her. "But I couldn't possibly make it for some hours yet."

"Oh dear, I don't think that will quite do."

She waited for me to change my mind, but voice or no, I knew I couldn't do it.

"I'm stuck here in the office," I explained. "Is there any chance you could come here?"

There was a pause while she considered this. I could understand her hesitation. This one didn't go to see men. They came to her, and in droves. There was probably a queue outside her door right now. Why should she disturb herself?

"Well," she said with evident reluctance, "I suppose I could. But it would have to be right away. Shall we say twenty minutes?"

We said twenty minutes, and I put down the phone. It didn't give me much time. The office would need redecorating, of course. I would have to get some new clothes, and maybe call in at the barbers. And La Digby would have to be told.

I went out to where she was busy typing.

"Mr. Thompson is on his way," she told me.

I'd forgotten him for the moment. Well, he'd better hurry up and get here. I didn't want Stella Raymond to see anybody like Thompson around the place. It might give her an entirely wrong impression of the organisation. Or worse, an entirely correct impression.

"Got a visitor coming," I announced importantly. "In twenty minutes. A Mrs. Stella Raymond. Please show her right in when she arrives."

Florence inspected me with narrowed eyes.

"My, my," she said crisply, "she must be something. You've been combing your hair."

I ignored this cheap sally, and went back to my newspaper. Almost at once Sam Thompson shambled in. He looked like last week's laundry, and was wearing most of it.

"Listen, Preston," he said, without preamble. "What is all this? I'm pretty busy right now, and I don't know if I can — "

"Too busy for fifty a day, plus expenses?" I cut in.

"Fifty?" He rubbed his chin. "I don't know, I have these bills, you see."

"Sixty then, and I'm being robbed. Here." I tossed over the telephone number Kurti had given me the night before. "Get a listing on that number. Find out the party's name, what he does for a living, all that stuff. And one more thing. For some reason, there's something special about certain times of the day. Two till three in the afternoon, six till seven in the evening. See if you can find out why."

He stared at the piece of paper.

"It'll mean cab-fare," he said carefully.

I peeled off two tens and a five and passed them to him. This caper was going to cost me a small fortune at this rate.

"For cabs," I told him nastily. "Don't let me catch you in any bars. This is important, Sam. Somebody might be trying to kill me."

"Oh dearie me," he replied. "Well, we can't have that, now can we? Tell you what, you go home and hide under the bed. I'll let you know when the nasty man goes away."

He grinned down at me, and one thing I have to give him. When Thompson grins, you grin back. He has that kind of face.

"Call me as soon as you have something. Time, as they say, is of the essence."

"And the sooner I get through with all this big detective work, the sooner I can get back to the good essence. See ya."

He went out, and I looked at my watch. Mrs. Raymond was due in less than ten minutes. The redecoration of the office would have to wait. So, too,

99

CITY LIBRARY CORK

would the redecoration of Preston. By the time I'd decided on the right angle for the ash-tray, my visitor had arrived.

Miss Digby opened the door and said, with a poker face, "Mrs. Raymond."

I stood up. All I'd had to go on was the voice, but everything else matched up. Jet-black hair, pulled clear of the finely chiselled features, showed off the deep tan of her skin, which carried almost no makeup. That skin didn't need it. She was tall, probably five eight, and moved with the athletic confidence of a thoroughbred. The simple cotton dress was beige-coloured and fell just below the knee, where straight brown legs ended in peep-toe sandals.

I didn't dare open my mouth in case my tongue lolled out.

"Good of you to see me, Mr. Preston."

She came in on a wave of good health and sea air, and the lightest

CITY LIBRARY CORK

touch of perfume. I swallowed hastily and took the outstretched hand.

"Please sit down, Mrs. Raymond."

Smiling, she seated herself, and turned her head to look quickly round the room. As she did so, I caught her profile, and almost gave myself away.

I'd seen that profile before.

It was the profile of the woman who had occupied the front seat of the helicopter on the trip back from Stavros Kurti's yacht.

6

STELLA RAYMOND had turned her head back towards me and was eyeing me speculatively. For the moment I felt confused, and it must have showed, but with luck she would accept that as a result of the impact she was accustomed to having on men.

"Do you smoke, Mrs. Raymond?"

I produced my Old Favorites, conscious that they weren't laid out in a silver box. She shook her head, smiling slightly.

"Thank you, no, but please do, if you wish. I like to see a man smoke."

Preferably from the ears, I added mentally, fooling around with the lighter.

"Well now, please tell me what I can do for you," I opened.

She waved a smooth brown arm towards the immaculate desk-top.

"Forgive me, Mr. Preston, but I understood over the telephone that you were too busy to leave the office."

There was just a hint of reproof in her tone, and I had to admit the question was fair.

"Phone calls," I explained. "There are a number of important telephone calls coming through, and I must be here to deal with them."

"Telephone, yes. Yes, of course." She considered this, then pouted slightly. "Your assistant outside struck me as a most efficient person. Could she not deal with these matters for you?"

I don't like to be cross-examined, not even by women who look like this one. My headshake was decisive.

"This is a one-man operation," I told her. "Highly confidential, and I'm the only person who really knows what's going on. Miss Digby is, as you say, most efficient. But when people hire me, they hire Preston, not an assistant.

Personal service is what they pay for, and I'm here to see they get it."

It sounded impressive, as I meant it to be. It seemed to mollify her.

"I see. Yes, I can understand that." She even managed a faint smile, which I gladly returned, and waited. My temporary confusion was under control now. It had dawned on me that there was just a chance she didn't realise we were old travelling companions. The man in the rear seat of the chopper had been hidden by a wig and a moustache. The whole thing had seemed a crazy charade at the time, but I was beginning to acquire a certain fondness for the anonymity provided. The point was, did this dark beauty know it had been me, and if not, what had led her to this office?

"Highly confidential I think you said, Mr. Preston?"

"Absolutely," I confirmed.

She nodded, tilting her head appraisingly to one side. Surely she must be able to hear my tail wagging?

"And any conversation we may have in this office would come under that heading?"

"If I was working for you, yes," I agreed.

"Ah. So we are talking about money."

There was just enough disdain in her voice to sting me into a reply.

"No. We are talking about a client relationship," I contradicted. "That is a legal definition of what transpires between a client and myself. It protects us both, in and out of a courtroom."

"Ah," she nodded. "Very well. I should like to become a client. How do we achieve that?"

"First," I explained, "I have to know what it is you want me to do. Then, I have to consider whether I'm going to do it. Perhaps you could tell me a little about the problem."

Her head was angled slightly away from me, and by half-closing my eyes I could visualise the night sky framed around her head, the way I'd seen it

105

the previous night. Unaware of the reference, she probably thought I was just staring at her. And maybe I was.

"This is very difficult," she began hesitantly, and broke off.

I was used to that. I've known some people beat around the bush for a whole hour before they could blurt out their troubles.

"Let's start at the beginning," I suggested. "The yellow pages are full of people like me. What made you pick this office?"

"That's easy. You picked yourself the moment you started looking for a certain person this morning."

Castanna. She couldn't be referring to anyone else.

"Just why would that be of interest to you, Mrs. Raymond?"

"Because he's blackmailing me," she jerked, between tight lips.

"Ah. Now blackmail is something I understand. A lot of my work hinges around it. People don't want the police involved, much less the newspapers and so forth, so they come to me."

Her eyes were pure olive as she looked into me.

' "And are you successful?" she queried.

"Mostly," I told her frankly. "Not always, but mostly. What is this blackmail about?"

"The usual thing," she replied with bitterness. "I was indiscreet, about a year ago. There are a few letters, and some photographs."

The usual thing, indeed. I was disappointed. For a woman to look like this one, and yet be dumb enough to get herself caught in that ancient trap was damaging to my image of her.

"I see," I returned smoothly. "And you are to pay out money, otherwise the — um — evidence will be shown to your husband."

To my surprise, she snorted.

"Him? I don't give a damn about him. For all I care, they can post the letters all round his bathroom. It's his lawyers I'm concerned about."

I nodded encouragingly, as though

that made everything perfectly clear. Experience told me that if I sat there long enough there would be more.

"Of course, that doesn't mean much to you, does it?" she muttered, half to herself.

"You were telling me about your husband's lawyers," I prompted.

"Lawyers," she scoffed. "Gangsters would be nearer the truth. It's just that they use briefs instead of machine-guns."

He'd heard much the same thing before, so it was scarcely original.

"You are involved then in some legal argument with your husband?"

If we kept things up at this rate, we might just get it all clear under an hour.

"It's the settlement," she explained. "We are divorced, you see, and under these damnable property laws he has a certain claim against my estate."

"And you against his," I pointed out reasonably.

"His?" she echoed with scorn. "His

108

estate consists of one spare toothbrush and a list of debts to every gambling casino within a hundred miles. This is a very one-sided settlement, Mr. Preston."

"I see. And, forgive my asking, but you are rather more favorably situated?"

She looked at me for a long moment, and a slow smile spread across the red mouth, which opened gradually to let the sun dance off gleaming teeth.

"Favorably situated?" she repeated. "I like that. Yes, I think I could claim to be. In point of fact, Mr. Preston, I am downright wealthy. Now do you see?"

I thought I did. The husband was a broker, and he was out to shake this dark beauty for every nickel he could get. This evidence, whatever it was, could be used against her.

"If I have it right," I replied, "your husband's lawyers would be able to use these papers to squeeze a bigger share out of you. But I don't quite see how, since you're already divorced."

"Then I'll explain. My husband, if you'll forgive the expression, is a thoroughly worthless creature. All he thinks about is women and gambling. I had no trouble in obtaining my divorce as the injured party, and as you must realise, that meant that his claims on my money would be minimal. This — um — development would be very welcome from his point of view. It does nothing for my image."

It was clearer now, and I settled back in my chair.

"So you have received this blackmail note — "

"No. There was no note. Just a telephone call."

"Right. A telephone call then. What were the instructions?"

"I was to take ten thousand dollars to a certain parking-lot. This Castanna person would hand over the package in exchange for the money. I went there, but he didn't keep the appointment. I know a few people down there, and

I asked about him. That's when they told me you were also looking for him. Could I ask why?"

I had to hand it to her. She was doing it all very well. If I hadn't spent some time in my fair-haired disguise I would probably have swallowed the whole tale. As it was, I still didn't know why she was involved, but one thing was clear. Stella Raymond wanted that briefcase, and if I could help her to trace it so much the better.

"Mrs. Raymond," I began slowly, "it begins to look as though we might be on the same team. I, too, had a telephone call from this man. In my case, he said he might be able to lead me to some stolen property, and there was a reward involved. That is very much in my line of business, so I arranged to see him. It seems to be his day for not keeping appointments."

We sat there, telling each other lies, and smiling. The only difference between us was that I knew my visitor was selling me a gold watch, whereas she thought I'd blundered into this by accident.

"What will you do now?" she enquired.

I shrugged.

"Probably nothing. These stolen property things happen all the time. I'm not disposed to waste much time on it. Besides, there's this new complication, and I don't want to get 'involved'."

"Complication?" she raised a finely arched brow. "You mean about my being blackmailed?"

If she was acting, she was good at it.

"No, Mrs. Raymond," I denied. "There's something else. It seems that Castanna had a partner. This partner got himself murdered during the night, and the police are very anxious to talk to our friend."

The shock on her face could not have been assumed.

"Murder? Castanna murdered someone?"

"Seems likely," I admitted. "And he

112

hasn't been keeping his appointments today."

"But this is terrible."

She wasn't talking to me. Ivory teeth were nibbling at her lower lip, while she absorbed what was evidently new information. On top of the shock, she had to rescramble her thinking to adjust to the new situation. If I'd wanted to hit her while she was down, I'd have asked her how it came about that her friends down at the beach forgot to mention the matter. A nice fresh murder is the kind of thing which is inclined to crop up in a conversation.

"This makes things worse," she said. "We have to find him and get those papers before the police catch him. Otherwise there's no telling where this will all end."

"We?" I echoed. "You did say 'we', Mrs. Raymond? Listen, I don't think I want to get involved in any murder case. The police can get very offhand about people meddling in their investigations."

She seemed to understand that. The words, anyway.

"I can well see that they might, and of course I would not ask you to do any such thing. My concern is with the letters. What happens to the man Castanna is of no interest to me. I rather hope they catch him. I don't like blackmailers, Mr. Preston. They are especially evil people. No," and she delved into the crocodile swing bag she'd carried in, "the murder aspect is a complication, but no more, as I see it. In fact, with the police now on the scene it becomes even more urgent that I should get my papers back before anyone else lays hands on them."

Producing a large manila envelope, she slid elegant fingers inside and pulled out a thick wad of currency bills. Then another, and another. I watched, mesmerised, as she placed these carefully in a row in front of me.

"That is the ten thousand dollars I was told to bring. Find my letters, Mr.

Preston. Whether you give that money to Castanna, or keep it yourself, is of no interest to me, so long as I get what I want."

It had to be bonanza week. Everybody kept giving me money. But my principles were offended. Stella Raymond hadn't said so, not in just so many words, but what she meant was that if I decided to hang on to the lot, bully for me. She would know that I might have to kill Castanna before he would part with the briefcase, and the thought didn't bother her at all. This was a lady who wanted what she wanted, and she wasn't about to be bothered with fine points of detail. Well, she'd picked the wrong man. If she thought she could just come into my office, waving those dollar bills, and I would do whatever she wanted, she was in for a disappointment. Right. A man has to stick to what is right, and my principles told me —

Reaching forward, I patted the wads of notes further to my side of the desk.

The hell with my principles.

"Let's suppose I get lucky, Mrs. Raymond. How do I deliver the goods?"

She gave me that lazy smile again. She'd had her own way, which was the only way she understood, and was now somehow more relaxed. I wondered just how relaxed she could get, and whether I would like to be around when she did it. The answer came up affirmative.

"In my experience," she said amusedly, "the people the world thinks of as lucky usually make their own luck. You strike me as being one of those people, Mr. Preston. I have a feeling you will succeed. You can contact me at this number. It's an apartment I keep at Beachside, and very few people know about it. It's what you might call my hideaway."

Nice hiding, I reflected, staring at the written address and telephone number. Beachside is millionaire country, and to be able to keep a place there just as a hideaway, Stella Raymond had to be very rich indeed.

"One thing," I reminded. "If this Castanna should get in touch with you, you'll let me know at once?"

She pouted.

"If necessary," she hedged. "I won't involve you if it might mean delay."

"The man is supposed to have killed already," I insisted. "You don't imagine he'd worry about increasing the tally, do you?"

We did the bit with the slingbag again, and I was hoping to see more money. It would have been a prettier sight than the blue-black thirty-two she waved at me.

"I'm not a fool," she assured me, "and I know how to use this."

Her tone and her posture were such that she wasn't going to listen if I argued.

"Very well. But please be careful."

The gun disappeared, and she tilted her head to one side in that provocative way of hers.

"Do you always worry so much about your clients?"

She was flirting with me, and the experience was painless.

"Just the women," I assured her.

"You have my address," she said, rising.

It was for me to decide whether she meant to refer to her status as a client or as a woman. I left the decision till later.

"I'll be in touch," I promised.

I walked her to the outer door, and watched with pleasure as she strode away down the corridor. Then I turned regretfully back, closing the door.

Florence Digby said, "The clientèle seems to be improving. Shall I bring my book?"

I knew that tone of old, with its overlay of disapproving approval. When we were seated in my own room, she sat with pencil poised, waiting. I'd already pushed the envelope containing the money into a drawer.

"The client's name," I began

importantly, "is Stella Raymond."

"I know all about Mrs. Raymond, thank you. All I need is the detail of the enquiry."

The interruption intrigued me, as she'd intended. And, if I wanted to know more, I was going to have to ask. As she'd also intended.

Sighing inwardly, I said, "All right, Florence, what is it you know about Mrs. Raymond?"

"Only what every woman's magazine has been carrying this past month," she informed me crisply. "Her divorce from Steve Raymond has been a godsend for the columnists."

I would have thought of it sooner had I not been so side-tracked by my new client's helicopter activities. Of course, she was *that* Mrs. Raymond. Steve Raymond had been the Man with the Golden Throat before he slid too much booze down it, when his record sales slid right alongside. One of my many deficiencies is my special technique for reading the newspapers. I devour the crime pages, then the sport pages, and that's the major reading done. Two more minutes are devoted to the international scene, to check that all my solutions for world problems are still valid. After that, I scrap the paper. I miss a lot of valuable information that way, and this Raymond business was typical. In future I would read everything with more care. Starting maybe tomorrow.

"I discontinued my subscription to most of the women's journals," I told Florence. "What do they have to say about our client?"

She sniffed, with that special sniff reserved for the wealthy or the famous, and in this case both.

"Well, to hear them tell it you would think he was entirely to blame. She's just a poor little rich girl. So they say. Of course, Steve Raymond has made his mistakes. You could scarcely wonder, with every woman in the country chasing after him. In that situation, one or two are bound to catch him, now aren't they?"

La Digby was making a joke, and that's a rare thing. I smiled in acknowledgement.

"I would say he was lucky," I admitted. "Of course, he could have stood still every now and then. Given the ladies a sporting chance. I think I might have."

Her look of withering scorn told me she had no illusions about the way I would behave.

"I don't think your version of Autumn in New York is quite in the Raymond class. Anyway, all the stories are slanted against him, and I think it's unfair. She probably owns all the magazines."

Nice piece of female reasoning.

"She'd have to be fairly wealthy. Where did she get all this money, anyway?"

She squinted at me suspiciously.

"Are you serious?"

"Certainly, yes."

"I would have thought everybody

knew that. From her father, of course. The man with the Midas touch. Some people say he's the richest man in the world. The big Turkish steamship owner, Stavros Kurti. Now, do you remember?"

But I wasn't listening any more. My mind was a jumble of information-pieces, sliding in and out of place, clicking, failing to connect, moving every which way.

Florence Digby was offended to be hustled out in quite such a hurry, but I needed to be alone.

One thing was transparently clear. Stavros Kurti had hired me to deliver a parcel. His daughter had hired me to locate the same piece of merchandise, but not for her dear old daddy.

The eighth richest man in the world was on the opposite side from his daughter, and in the middle was the briefcase.

And me.

7

WHEN the phone interrupted my unhappy reverie I didn't answer at once. There hadn't been time to adjust to my new position. Once I told the caller that I'd lost the case the momentum might be taken over by the massive forces at Kurti's command, and that was not a prospect I could face with any relish. It wasn't that I was afraid exactly, but I felt entitled to a measure of apprehension.

Finally, I picked up the jangling intruder and muttered a hoarse, "Hallo."

"Preston?"

Sam Thompson's voice had never sounded so pleasing.

"Yes, Sam, what have you got?"

"You got a sore throat or something? Listen, I have to be careful of my sinuses."

"Never mind your health problems, and no, I haven't got a sore throat. What did you find out?"

"This number you gave me," he replied, "it's a real high-class operation, am I right?"

"Could be," I said carefully. "What's the listing?"

"If there is one, it's probably under citizens and taxpayers or something. It's a pay phone, corner of Crane and Conquest."

Great.

"Is there a coffee bar or anything like that, where you could sit and watch the booth?"

"Ha-ha. Coffee bar? Listen, have you been down there lately? It's all sex aids and blue movies. Even the slot-machine parlour has a video section. A man could pick up bad habits. Surveillance you want? I'll need a car."

I hesitated. This thing was costing me real money. If Kurti shouted for his fee back, and I could scarcely blame him, I could wind up in debt. I didn't count in Stella Raymond's ten thousand. As far as I was concerned, that stuff was just passing through.

"All right, Sam. Hire yourself a car. A small one. Be sure you have a clear view of the booth between two o'clock and three. If nothing happens, get back to me, I may have something else for you. Particularly now that you're mobile."

He grunted something about tight-wad employers, and hung up. I felt suddenly exposed. This sitting around, waiting for the unknown Ramondez to call, was no way out of the trouble that was heading in my direction. I ought to be out and around, asking questions, banging heads. True enough, I was obeying orders by staying put, but that was before anything went wrong. After all, I reasoned, what was going to happen when the call came through? I was going to pass out the bad news, and Ramondez was going to consider what to do next. Usually, when people try to analyse situations, what they're really doing is to marshal the facts in such a way that they point to the course of action they have already decided to follow anyway. I'm no different from the next man. I picked over the facts, and came up with the answer I wanted.

Stavros Kurti had entrusted me with his goods, and I'd lost them. He'd paid me a lot of money, and that I still had. For what? For what? So that I could answer telephone calls? No. People don't pay out that kind of money for message boys. They pay it on an assumption of initiative and resource. He knew about me before he gave me the job. He wouldn't expect me to be sitting on my butt, waiting for teacher to tell me what to do. He would expect me to be out there, poking around, looking for his parcel. He was paying for results, not excuses.

That was the answer I'd been working towards, and the one I wanted to hear. The moment I reached it, I headed for the door. Florence turned towards me, waiting.

"A man named Ramondez may call," I told her. "It's very important. Tell him there's been a development, and I've had to go out. You don't know when I'll be back."

"Is there a number where he could reach you?"

"No," I decided. "I'll be moving around all over. But I have a number where I can call him. Tell him I'll call as soon after two o'clock as I can."

She nodded.

"Ramondez. Two o'clock. Anything else?"

I'd almost forgotten Stella Raymond's ten thousand in my anxiety to get away. A man ought not to be careless about such details.

"There are two lots of money in the office," I said. "Ten thousand and five thousand. Cash makes me nervous, what with all the terrible things you read in the papers. Take it to the bank, will you, and put it in a strong-box."

It's nice to be able to surprise her sometimes.

"Fifteen thousand dollars?" she queried. "Where did you get it all?"

"I'm working for a guy named Midas," I assured her solemnly.

"Midas only worked in gold," she objected.

"This is the paper branch of the family. And it's easier to steal."

"Very well, I'll lock it up," she affirmed. "Er, I suppose the use of the strong-box indicates that you don't expect to keep it very long?"

"Just looking after it for a friend."

"She has very good legs, your friend," she shot out venomously.

"That so? I didn't notice."

The Digby sniff is in a class by itself. I could still hear it as I waited for the elevator.

The doors slid smoothly open, and a man stepped out. I moved inside, and felt a tap on the arm.

"Excuse me, but it is Mr. Preston, isn't it? Mr. Mark Preston?"

Reluctantly, I turned to look at him. Until then he'd been just a man coming out of an elevator. Now, he was a man asking who I was, and such people get looked at. Fair hair, clipped short, surmounted a smooth round face which held questioning eyes. His five feet ten inches were packed inside a lightweight blue non-crease suit. Soft white shirt and a tie of quiet blue wool completed the picture. He radiated an air of non-assertive confidence and authority, as he waited, half-smiling, for my reply. He was the complete corporation man, but what corporation? He could be big business, government or mob. As the three great institutions grew more alike in approach and methods, so their outriders began to look more and more alike in appearance.

"I'm Preston," I confirmed. "And you?"

"Splendid," he assured me cheerfully. "I was just coming to get you."

That didn't sound good at all. If only the elevator doors would close,

I could leave him standing there. But they couldn't do that, not with him leaning on the button. What did he mean, get me?

"What do you mean, get me?" I said it out loud.

"Let me introduce myself. I'm Hawkins, Internal Revenue. My authority."

I stared at his identification carefully. It looked authentic enough.

"Well, you don't need me, Mr. Hawkins," I bluffed. "My secretary takes care of all that tax stuff. She'll be glad to show you over the books. Nice to have met you."

I stared meaningly at his finger, which remained glued to the button. Hawkins shook his head.

"I'm not a tax-man," he informed me. "Not in the narrow sense. I'll explain it all to you when we get down to the office."

It seemed to me he took too damn much for granted.

"I haven't time right now," I said curtly. "Glad to co-operate, and all that stuff, but I'm busy. Call me, and we'll fix up an appointment."

There was an extra touch of flint in the eyes now.

"It has to be now, Mr. Preston. You don't want a lot of nonsense with uniforms and sirens, do you? So undignified."

Let us not be undignified, I thought sourly. I shrugged.

"Well, if it won't take too long."

He smiled and came in beside me. We didn't speak after that, not even as he drove expertly through the busy late-morning traffic, pulling up outside an office block. He led the way inside, and up to sixteen. The legend on the door read 'Acme Toys and Games'. I read it with alarm, but he said, "Don't worry about the sign. The place belongs to my uncle. And yours."

The only uncle we could possibly have in common was my dear old Uncle Sam, and the office didn't say much for his status. It was just one room, almost bare of trappings.

Certainly there was no sign of any office work being done there.

"Have a seat, Mr. Preston."

There were three visitors' chairs, plain straight-backed wooden items. I sat facing the battered desk, behind which Hawkins now parked himself on worn leather. Opening a drawer, he pulled out a thin blue folder and opened it.

"You're an interesting man, Mr. Preston," he offered. "There's some kind of reference to you in almost every official agency."

That could be good, or not good.

"I wouldn't have thought I was that important," I said non-committally.

Hawkins looked up from the papers, frowning slightly.

"I didn't say you were important," he corrected. "I said interesting. Something of an enigma, too. You seem to manage to stay about one jump ahead of the police in your various doings. A little bit illegal, a little bit dishonest, always operating inside some curious set of rules of your own making. You get results, too, by all accounts. Chiefly because you don't hold yourself bound too much by pettifogging detail, such as the law of the land."

"It's your office," I returned evenly, "so you can make snide remarks and get away with it. I'm just a guest here. They always told me the guest shouldn't contradict the master of the house. Just what is it you want, Mr. Hawkins? I don't know much about toys or games."

He tapped lightly on the folder with well-scrubbed fingers.

"You're too modest," he reproved. "My information is that you are strong in the games area. Don't play games with me, Mr. Preston, or I will squash you like a bug on a wall."

If he'd blustered or shouted, I could have ridden it. But he made it a plain statement, delivered with bland good humour, and the effect was chilling. I know what these government people can get away with if they feel the common security is at threat.

"You're going too fast for me," I said, and I tried to sound calm.

"Then I'll slow it down. A number of agencies are involved here. If you read the papers you will probably have the impression that we all blunder around in the dark, and never talk to one another. To start with, you can correct that. We try to keep in touch as much as we can, and for obvious reasons. This little matter today, for instance, is of great interest to a number of people. I hope you won't think I'm name dropping when I tell you who they are. The Treasury, the F.B.I., the Immigration Bureau. There are others, but I need not bother you with those. I think you will have quite enough to think about, with the departments I've mentioned."

He was right there. The only people he'd left out were the Marines. Unless he was lying to me — and why should he? — the man talking to me represented about as much big trouble as it was possible to muster.

"So I'm impressed," I admitted, "but it seems like a big team to turn out against one harmless citizen. What did I do, blow up the White House? I forget."

He leaned back, nodding.

"Your third-grade sense of humor is on the record," he replied, unmoved. "Try keeping it in your pocket for now. Do you know this man? And think hard before you reply."

I found myself inspecting a foto-fit picture of a man's head. He was about thirty years old, broad-faced and had a mop of fair hair, and a generous moustache. He looked pretty much the way I must have looked the previous night, except that the nose was too broad, and he was obviously a few years younger. Prolonging the moment as long as I could, I held it at all kinds of angles, finally shaking my head.

"I don't think so," I muttered, as though to myself.

"You're sure?" he pressed.

Time for the open frankness bit.

"Well no," I wriggled. "I couldn't be sure, not to take an oath, that is. But just on looking at this made-up sketch, no, I don't think I know him. Maybe if you could put something distinctive on him, like a uniform. Maybe if the picture was full-length, you know, to kind of fill him out. As it is — "

I shrugged and put the drawing back on the desk.

"You're not working with him, then?"

I could afford to look surprised.

"I don't work with anybody. Read the file. This is a one-man operation, it says so on the door."

"I don't give a damn what it says on the door, and don't be evasive with me."

Hawkins was probably a lovable man at home, but he was at his place of work now.

"I'm not being evasive," I said reasonably. "You ask me if I know this man, and I tell you no. You ask

136

if he's working with me, and I tell you no. What's evasive?"

He did some more finger-drumming. It was quite rhythmic, in a staccato kind of way.

"You've been haring up and down the waterfront, banging on doors, asking questions. You've stuck your nose into a murder case, misled a senior dock security officer, generally been about as subtle as a sailor on a twelve-hour pass. I want to know what you're up to, and let me make one thing very plain. If I don't like your story, you'll be taken somewhere else to try again. This office may not be much to look at, but believe me, it's the promised land when you compare it with some of the places we ask questions. You have the floor, and I advise you not to waste my time."

That was bad news indeed. Hawkins was not bluffing, and with all those other agencies rooting for him I could be in a great deal of trouble. These people were not the police. With the police, a man has a fighting chance. There are such things as rights, and lawyers, and all the paraphernalia of the legal system. All that went out the window when these other people came in the door.

The man opposite waited while I tried to unscramble my thinking. It was too late in the day for me to come up with some new story. If I tried the one about the fishing-trip he'd be hollering for his rubber truncheon before I got half-way through. The one about the stolen property was better, not good, but better. Resisting the impulse to cross my fingers, I told him the tale about Castanna having telephoned me.

He didn't like it too well, and he asked a lot of questions, but at least he wasn't hand-drumming. I had the feeling he'd heard the story before, and obviously he'd been talking to some of the people I'd been in touch with.

"Why did you tell Inspector Cutter

this nonsense about a fishing-trip?" he challenged.

"Oh come on," I replied knowingly. "The man was all on edge. He was dying to get his hands on somebody, anybody, so he could shift that spotlight away from himself. If I'd told him I was committing a felony, he'd have hollered murder, and — "

"Felony? What felony?" snapped my interrogator.

"Withholding information about stolen property," I told him blandly. "That may not be much of a crime, but believe me, it would have been enough for Cutter."

"You're telling me about it," he pointed out. "Why shouldn't I have you locked up?"

"C'm on, Hawkins, be your age," I risked. "Here's you and all those bigfish government people out on some whalehunt. You don't have time to stop for minnow."

"You're taking a chance, telling me this."

"Not much of one, I fancy. Big operators think big. You're not interested in trivial offenses."

I seemed to have struck the right note. Hawkins was not the man to let his face reveal anything, but there was a general easing in his posture, as some of the tension went out of him.

"Let's assume for the moment that I haven't time to bother with your little misdemeanours. What will you do next?"

That was easy.

"I'll get the hell out of here as fast as I can, and have a large Scotch on the rocks. Then I'll get on with what I was doing."

"You mean looking for Castanna?" he queried, surprised.

"Sure, why not? If he has something to sell, I want to know what it is. Could be a reward, and with people like you involved, the reward could be big. It'll be easier now."

"How easier?"

I tapped at the foto-fit picture.

"Now that I know what he looks like," I explained. "That always helps a lot."

"Huh."

His reaction was to make a short explosive noise, and relax back in his chair.

"Huh," he repeated. "You mean I haven't scared you off?"

"You could scare me off, and fast, if you wanted to," and I meant every word. "But you haven't tried. You haven't threatened me, you haven't even waved a finger. Therefore, deduction. You don't much care what I do so long as I don't get in your way. Right?"

He even managed a small smile at that.

"Almost," he concurred. "You're almost right. But I think I'd better give you a little idea of what's going on here, so that you'll know what you're up against."

Confidence, yet — it was a gesture, and I appreciated it. I even offered him an Old Favorite. He refused, but I didn't.

"I shall pay very close attention," I assured him.

"Let's start with him," and he pointed to the sketch.

"Castanna?"

"Wrong," he contradicted, and with some satisfaction. "This is not him. This man is the one we shall call the third party. Besides, you are supposed to have seen the real Castanna. You gave Inspector Cutter a description, remember?"

He'd saved that one, as a kind of sucker punch, and I was lucky to be able to catch it.

"Look," I said reasonably, "I've already admitted I told that man a tale to get him off my back. Description? He asked me to describe two men, so that's what I did. Read what I told him. They could have been any two guys off the street. He wasn't really paying attention, because he knew what he wanted to hear, and it suited him to

142

have my description fit. If either one of those men had had some distinguishing feature, like a scarred face, or a limp or something, he'd have cottoned on to me right away, because I didn't mention it. My so-called description would fit any two men. Read it."

To an ordinary man, my explanation would have been unconvincing. But Hawkins was a trained investigator, a professional. The years had taught him how much reliance to place on descriptions supplied by witnesses. He would know, too, the temptation of the investigating officer, which is to accept a description as applying to someone that suited him.

"All right, I'll go along with that, for the moment. Tell you the truth, Preston, I don't know what kind of security man he is, but when it comes to homicide, Cutter is a first-day apprentice."

It was a concession. It put Hawkins and me on the same team. And it made me even more wary. The Revenue man was smooth in more places than his unlined cheeks. They say sharks give you a kind of smile before the big bite, and this was shark country I was in.

But I grinned like a conspirator, and he carried on.

"What does the name Stavros Kurti mean to you?"

I frowned, thinking.

"Big shipping man?" I volunteered. "Owns about half the world, and most of the women. What about him?"

"He is in a lot of trouble with our government. You probably read something about it in the papers."

"Sure, I read something about it," I agreed. "Big international scandal or something. I don't bother with the details. The papers are always full of crap when they get a big name to play with. It'll all die down. It always does. Nothing ever happens to these people, not the big ones."

He listened to this piece of man-in-the-street philosophy, then nodded.

"That's about the reaction we would

normally expect. Only this time it's wrong. This time, he could be in real trouble. My job is to supply the trouble. I can see by your face that you're sceptical about my chances. Would it surprise you to know that Kurti is already afraid to enter the country, that he's staying fixed on a yacht out there?" — and he waved in the general direction of the ocean.

"Then why don't you just go out and get him?" I asked innocently.

"Because he's just outside our jurisdiction," he explained patiently. "In international waters. He's up to something, and we want to know what it is. There are people here, working on his behalf — lawyers, businessmen, all kinds of people. Money is no object with Mr. Kurti. If there's a loophole in the law, they will find it. And if there isn't, they'll make one. That's why I have to know what he's doing here. Now, this man — " and we were back to the picture again — "could be some kind of messenger. He went out to the ship last night. We know that, because we had this description sent."

"Deduction," I interrupted, "you have a man in the crew."

"Never mind that. This messenger came back ashore carrying a briefcase he didn't have when he arrived. I want that case."

"And the man, naturally," I asked.

"He doesn't interest me, except that he had the case. He's no one important, that much I know. Kurti wouldn't risk anyone who mattered in case they should be under surveillance. He's right, at that."

It doesn't do anything for a man's morale to hear himself being dismissed as someone who doesn't matter.

"But he couldn't be just any joe," I objected, "not if someone like Kurti dealt with him personally."

"Oh no, that's true," he admitted. "It would have to be somebody reliable, somebody Mr. Kurti was prepared to trust."

I felt somewhat mollified after that concession.

"So he's the man to find," I said, thoughtfully.

Hawkins shook his head.

"I doubt it," he contradicted. "It's my suspicion that this man is already dead."

"Dead? What makes you think that?"

"It fits everything else. Our Third Party was taken out by launch to see Kurti. But he didn't come back that way, he came by helicopter."

"Fancy travelling," I interjected, but he looked annoyed at the interruption.

"There were two other men on the launch. Castanna was one, and a man named Street was the other. Something happened between them, and Castanna killed Street. What took place after that is only conjecture at this stage, but this we do know. Castanna has something for sale, and it's a reasonable assumption that he's offering the briefcase."

I had an objection to that.

"But you said the Third Party came back on a chopper."

"Yes, but not to the airport. Much too public. He would have been dropped somewhere out of town, a football stadium, a race-track, anywhere that's flat. And from there he would need a car. Somebody had to drive it, or at least supply it, and I'm betting on Castanna. He would have no idea what the briefcase contained, in all probability, but he's not a fool. When a man is taken in secrecy to see someone like Stavros Kurti, and then comes back carrying something, that something has to be valuable."

It was unnerving the way Mr. Smooth-Faced Hawkins could cut his way through the undergrowth to come up with the right answers.

"Well, assuming you're right, and I don't know enough to have any better ideas," I said modestly, "Why should Castanna come to me?"

He beamed then, and it changed his whole appearance.

"Ah yes," he returned joyfully, "why indeed? Because you bring the whole affair into workaday perspective. No government here. No international finance, no gigantic multimillion swindle. Just a common sneak-thief trying to unload some stolen property. And where would he take it, in Monkton City? There are only three or four people who would know how to deal with such a situation. People with a history of recovering stolen items at a price. I don't want to hurt your feelings, Mr. Preston, but you are one of those people. A logical choice, if I may say so."

Personally, I would have preferred a more flattering background. He could have said something about my good standing with the law, for example. Or, he could have mentioned the time and trouble I save everybody, bringing about these reunions between stolen property and the losers thereof. I felt that his summation lacked polish.

All the same, it gave me an

unquestioned place in the game, and I ought to be grateful for that.

"Are you warning me off?"

"No. Definitely not. Quite the reverse, in fact. I want you to go right ahead. I know how you work, you see. Blundering around, asking questions, punching heads, generally making yourself a nuisance, until something breaks. Crude, but effective. You get results, and that is what we want. Get that briefcase."

I looked doubtful, and not without reason.

"Look, I'm not sure about this. You people have everything going for you. Organisation, computers, money. To say nothing of manpower. Besides, this Castanna already killed two people. This looks to me like a job you could handle much better. It's beginning to make me feel nervous."

He looked unimpressed.

"You've dealt with killers before," he said snidely. "Besides, you have nothing to fear from Castanna. So far as he's concerned you're the money-man. Nobody kills the money-man. As to the organisation, yes, I have all that. But we all have to operate in great secrecy. Kurti is remarkably well informed on everything we do, and this is a vast undercover exercise. What we need here is the old-fashioned blunt instrument, one that has no official connections. You fit the description very nicely."

It isn't every day a man gets cut down to size. Blunt instrument, forsooth.

"Suppose I won't do it?"

I'd been right about those sharks. They do smile just before the big bite.

"Then I regret that you will face about seventeen different criminal charges, state and federal. Would you like the list?"

I didn't want to see any list. I could think of a few off the cuff, which were legitimate. The Lord alone knew how many others this character could invent, and make them stick.

"Will there be a reward?"

"Of course," he assured me. "What greater reward can a man have than the thanks of a grateful government?"

"Suppose I get killed?" I queried.

He made deprecatory hand-movements.

"If anything should happen to you, I should feel it very deeply."

"I'll bet."

He gave me a number where I could reach him, and told me to keep in touch. I was glad to get out of there.

There was one thing Mr. Smartass Hawkins did not yet know. One thing I would have had the devil of a job to explain away. He hadn't yet learned that Stella Raymond had called on me. Well, he was ahead of me in every other department. It was only fair that I should be left with something up my sleeve.

Downstairs, I looked at my reflection in the revolving door.

Blunt instrument indeed.

8

IT was precisely two o'clock when I dialled the number Kurti had given me. I listened to it ringing for almost a minute before a voice said softly, "Hallo?"

"This is the delivery service," I said carefully. "I'm calling about a certain parcel."

I don't like to play games, but when a public telephone rings, anyone is liable to pick it up.

The man at the other end came back, "Was this parcel delivered by sea?"

There was a thick Spanish accent to the words, and I wondered whether I was talking to the man who was supposed to be giving me instructions.

"Yes, there was a sea trip involved. Is this Señor Ramondez?"

"*Si*, yes, I am Esteban Ramondez," he confirmed, after some hesitation.

"Why do you call here? Why do you not wait?"

This was the part I did not relish. Nobody likes to admit failure, and to have to do so to a total stranger did not make it any more enjoyable.

"Fact is, señor, there's been kind of a hitch."

"Hitch? What is this hitch?"

It wasn't clear whether he was asking for the details, or whether he didn't know what the word meant.

"Things have gone wrong," I admitted. "The parcel is missing."

"Missing? You must explain, please."

"On my way home last night I was attacked and robbed. The parcel was taken. I've an idea who might be responsible, and I'm looking for him right now."

So were half the police in town, but I didn't want to make things worse than they already were, so I kept quiet about that.

"This is very bad news, señor. Bad for me, bad for you. I do not think my

154

employer will like this news."

That had the hollow ring of a death sentence. Whatever spirits I had left sank even lower.

"I just need a little time," I assured him. "I'm confident I can straighten this out."

"My employer does not like complications," he told me quietly. "You were given a very simple task. I must now tell him you have failed."

"Couldn't you delay that, just for a little while?" I urged. "I'm sure I can get to the bottom of it."

He turned me down flat.

"I have no authority. I must report to my employer. You will remain in your office for further instructions."

That didn't suit me at all. I wasn't going to achieve anything sitting behind a desk. Everybody else involved in this caper was out there on the street, moving around, doing things. My place was with them, if I ever hoped to get anything done.

"No," I refused. "I have several

leads, and I must follow them up now. I shall call this number again at six o'clock."

He sighed.

"You must understand, señor, that if you refuse to do as I ask I cannot be held responsible for anything that may happen."

I could almost hear him washing his hands.

"You can tell our employer," emphasising the 'our', "that I have my own methods. I have to try to put things right. I'll call at six."

"Very well."

He broke the connection, and I replaced the receiver. I didn't envy Señor Ramondez. This whole foul-up might be my doing, but at least I'd only had to admit it to a third party. He had the job of telling the number one boss man, and he was welcome to it.

Florence Digby tapped at the door.

"I didn't interrupt while you were on the phone," she explained, "but there's a man outside who wants to see you."

It was evident from her tone that she didn't have a very high opinion of my visitor.

"What kind of man?"

"A roughish sort of person. His name's Street."

I got interested all at once. It was the same name as my escort of the previous night, the man presumably murdered by Castanna.

"Show him in, Florence."

She shrank as close to the door as she could get as she waved him inside. A girl doesn't want to get too close to roughish persons.

He was short and stocky, with a round face which would look cheerful under normal circumstances. The clothes were those of a man who worked with his hands. I stood up to greet him, because he looked somewhat lost, standing there and staring around.

"What can I do for you, Mr. Street?"

When he spoke, there was a gentle rasp to his voice, which was not unpleasant on the ear.

"I'm Darrel Street," he announced. "Burt's brother."

"Take a seat."

He sat down awkwardly on the chair Stella Raymond had vacated a few hours before. Appearance-wise, it was no contest.

"Thought we ought to get together," he blurted out. "You're looking for Angelo Castanna. Me too. Thought we ought to, like, get together."

If he was going to repeat everything, at least I'd have no problems about his meaning.

"And if we do?" I questioned. "What happens when we find him?"

He looked at me in astonishment.

"Do? Why, I'm going to kill him, is what."

He would, too. Looking at his eyes, and the set of his jaw, I had no doubt of his sincerity.

"Mr. Street — " I began.

"Del," he interrupted. "Call me Del. Everybody does."

"Del, then. I advise you not to be

too hasty about this. The law — "

"Law? Huh. What'll they do? He'll get some greasy lawyer and wind up with one to three. A year from now he'll be out and walking around. My brother won't. He'll be just as dead then as he is now. Don't waste my time with no law. Let's just find the murdering little bastard, and kill him."

With the advent of agent Hawkins, I had assumed the only missing ingredient to be the U.S. Marines. I'd forgotten about the vigilantes, and now here they were, right in my own office.

"Del, let's talk for a minute," I began.

"I ain't too good on talking," he objected. "Besides, what's to talk about? Just get on and do it, that's my beat."

"Believe me, I can understand the way you feel. Your brother is dead, and you want revenge. Nothing could be more natural."

"Well, then?"

"Nothing could be more natural," I

repeated insistently, "than to want to get back at the man responsible. But first we have to be sure who that man is."

Del Street looked perplexed.

"We know who it is. It's Castanna, that's who it is."

"We don't know anything of the kind," I corrected.

I was confusing him now, as I'd intended.

"Listen, the whole waterfront — "

" — the whole waterfront is full of crap," I cut in sharply. "Those people down there don't have the slightest idea what's coming off here. What they don't know, they invent."

He listened, at least I'd achieved that much.

"You know different, huh?" he queried, with some scorn.

"I know more than they do," I assured him. "They have this down as some kind of drunken brawl, don't they? A fight starts, and one man kills the other. Yes?"

His nod was reluctant.

"Something like that. Anyway, what's the difference?"

"The difference is, there's much more to it. There's something big involved here. I don't know what it is, not yet, but people have been waving money at me to find out."

"Yeah?" He was wide-eyed now. "What kinda people?"

"People who can afford it, that's all I can tell you. They have a theory that whoever killed your brother is also trying to kill Castanna, and that's why he's hiding. Now do you see?"

He ought to, I reasoned. It was quite a plausible little story, when you consider I made it up in no seconds flat. The mental turmoil this created inside my visitor manifested itself by a jerky crossing and uncrossing of his legs as he swung from side to side on the chair.

"You wouldn't kid me, would you?"

"I've been offered real money," I evaded, "thousands of dollars, in fact.

That doesn't happen after a fight between two drunks."

It was the kind of reasoning he would follow. Nodding slowly, he said, "No. That's right enough. It don't. But who else would want to rub out old Burt? And something big, you say? Like what?"

At least he was talking, and that's an old axiom. So long as people are talking, they're not fighting. Or killing.

"One thing at a time. Let's talk a little about your brother. What kind of man was he?"

"Burt? Burt is — was — great. I got kids, you know. You should ask them about their Uncle Burt. Why, every time he comes home he's around the house, always presents for everybody."

"He's away a lot, then?"

There was suspicion on his face now.

"Don't you know nothing about him at all?"

"Not a thing," I assured him.

"Oh." And he seemed satisfied.

"Well, Burt used to be kind of wild, when he was younger. But these past eight years he's settled down just fine. He likes his job, he gets well paid, sees the world. Got it made, you might say."

Something told me we were beginning to make progress.

"What job was that?"

"Jevver hear tell of a guy named Kurti? Everybody knows him, he's got more money than Fort Knox. Well, Burt works — worked for him. What they call personal crew, I mean. This Kurti, he employs thousands of guys, probably never laid eyes on half of them, but Burt was special. There's a few called personal crew. Burt's one of those."

"And he's away a lot?"

"What else? He's a seaman, ain't he? That's what seamen do, they go away."

I was thinking about a certain ship called the *Monkton Pride*, and a sweater that turned up in a boat manned by a sailor who was away a lot. A sailor who was personal crew to the owner of the shipping line which collected heavy insurance on the loss of the *Pride*. Burton Street began to sound like a very interesting sailor indeed.

"Did Burt ever talk about his work? I mean, could there be something to learn there? Somebody he might have upset enough for them to want to kill him?"

"Nah," he rejected. "Everybody liked Burt. He kept himself to himself, after he settled down. Who'd want to hurt him?"

I tried another tack.

"Was he married?"

Del looked uncomfortable, and when he replied he wouldn't look at me direct.

"No. He couldn't, you see. He was — was — stuck on this lady. A married party. I used to try to snap him out of it, but he wouldn't be told. It wasn't as if she'd even look at him. He was just one more guy worked for her old man."

"Her old man? You mean Burt was in love with Mrs. Kurti?"

"Not that kind of old man. I mean her father. It was Kurti's daughter he was stuck on. The whole thing was crazy from the start. But you know how it is when a man gets the big one. If he picks the wrong dame, he's got grief."

And Burton Street had certainly picked the wrong dame, I reflected. Just about as wrong as he could find. As to the grief, well, he was certainly dead. This new information from his brother Del had started several new trains of thought in.

Up until a few minutes ago, Burt had been little more than an anonymous corpse. Suddenly, he had become a very interesting man. I wanted to know more about him. The man who could help me best was sitting on the other side of the desk. Always provided I could talk him into it.

165

"I think your brother can help us," I said seriously.

Del was confused again, but he was listening.

"How help us? He's dead, ain't he? What's your pitch?"

"Up until now, everybody has been thinking the way you've been thinking. Burton Street is dead. Find Angelo Castanna, and that'll be the end of it. Just another waterfront flare-up. I don't believe that. I think there's more to it, a whole lot more."

"Even if you're right," he returned doubtfully, "I don't see how Burt — "

"Where was he living? Do you have an address?"

"Sure. He always stayed the same place when he was home. Nice place, not your usual flop. Burt was always neat, you know."

Better and better.

"I want you to go there, Del, sniff around. You have the right, as next of kin."

"Why would I want to do that? I was

166

going to leave all that kind of stuff to the wife."

"Don't," I urged. "She won't know what to look for."

"Her and me both," he said obstinately.

In my anxiety, I'd been forgetting that this was a man who needed everything spelling out.

"I think your brother was involved in something," I explained. "What you'll be doing is trying to find out what it was."

I'd started badly, as his face immediately showed.

"Oh no," he rejected. "What kind of a heel d'you think I am? My own brother? He's not even in his grave yet, and you want me to lay some kind of stuff on him? You're creepy, you know that?"

"You're going to have to make up your mind what you really want, Del," I told him gently. "We have to know what Burt was up to before we can find out who killed him. You can protect his good name, that's your right. But you will probably be protecting his killer at the same time. Do you want revenge, or not?"

He went into that leg-shuffling routine again, while he brought his mind to bear on this new problem.

"Suppose I did this, and I ain't saying I will, what would I be looking for?"

"Anything that might give us a lead. He wouldn't have kept any diary, I shouldn't imagine, but there could be other stuff. Addresses, telephone numbers. You might find pawn tickets, bank pass-books, anything like that. Oh, and keys. Watch out for anything that could be a lead to a safe-deposit box, a bus-station locker, anything of that kind."

"Or letters, maybe?" he suggested. Evidently the idea was sinking in, and I nodded quickly.

"You got it," I agreed. What'll I do if I find something?"

"Let me know, and we'll follow it up

together. I don't advise you to strike out on your own. Don't forget that whoever killed your brother is still out there. They wouldn't hesitate to give you the same treatment, not if they thought you were getting close."

The mention of danger challenged his manhood at once.

"Listen, they can try, I sure hope they do. Darrel Street knows how to handle himself, you bet."

"I don't doubt it," I assured him quickly. "You'd be a good man in a brawl, and I'd sooner have you with me than against me. But this isn't that kind of show-up. This is a knife in the back, a bullet from a closed car. The man hasn't been born who can protect himself against that kind of stuff. These people work in the dark. Under cover. We have to do the same, if we're going to get them. Do you see?"

He didn't like it, but I was getting through to him.

"Well," he grumbled, "I guess so. Why don't you come down there with me? You'd know better what to look for."

I shook my head vehemently.

"Can't do that. The police are watching me already. Maybe the opposition too, for all I know. Nobody's watching you. You're his brother, the surviving relative. It's only natural you should take charge of his belongings. In fact, it would look suspicious if you didn't. You can see that, can't you?"

His face cleared at last, and I knew the decision was made.

"O.K. I'll do it. Let you know what I find. But you have to do something for me."

"Name it."

"If you turn up anything that tells you who murdered my brother, you tell me. I didn't come here to solve no crimes. I come to get the bastard who did it to him. So?"

"Agreed. And if the police get talking to you, don't mention my name. It won't help you, and it certainly won't help me."

He stood up, hesitated for a moment, then stuck out his hand.

"We'll get 'em, right?"

His hand was rough and firm.

"We'll do our best, Del," I promised him.

When he went out, I sat thinking about this development, and speculating about what he might find at his dead brother's apartment. Probably nothing, I decided. The important thing had been to divert Darrel Street from his main-street-at-sundown shenanigans. He'd only get himself killed, and there was no point in that. There was also no point in my sitting around the office.

It was time I paid a call on a certain lady.

9

IN my section of the woods, three o'clock on a summer afternoon means hot. Like very. People move around slowly, if at all. Even the traffic drops into a lethargic low-gear kind of crawl. The whole effect is something like watching a picture in slow motion. The expressions on the actors' faces become glassy and fixed, almost zombie-like. I was no better than the rest as I drove steadily down to Beachside. My collar began to crumple as soon as I got in the car, and was well into its white string impersonation by the time I parked.

In this desirable residential section, the view was the same they showed you on the movies, on the day after the bomb dropped. There was no sign of life, all shutters were shuttered, and the place was a ghost town. The only thing lacking was that lost and hungry dog they always have, padding hopelessly around.

The address Stella Raymond had given me turned out to be a revelation. It was as if the architect, instead of drawing up plans of his own, had simply bought a two-hundred-year-old place in old Spain, and shipped it over, stone by stone. Instead of steel and concrete, there were elegant curves and arches, a timeless blending of white stone and black ironwork. The main entrance was a simple, wrought-iron gate leading into a passageway, which emerged into a large courtyard.

Here, the design was such that little daylight penetrated. A large fountain shushed gently away in the middle, while lush semi-tropical vegetation flourished on all sides. It was quiet here, quiet and cool and timeless. For my part I'd have been content to sit by the fountain and watch the water play for an hour. Or a day, perhaps. It was that kind of setting.

I took a regretful look at the scene, and got back to business. All the apartments led off from the courtyard, and it was a simple matter to walk around the walls until I found the number I'd been given. There was an ancient handbell which the visitor had to pull to announce arrival. I gave it a yank, and heard a musical jangle from somewhere inside. After a while, the door opened, and the lady I'd come to see stood looking at me. I returned the compliment, and was getting much the better of the deal. She'd piled up her hair since we last met, accentuating the long curve of her neck, and highlighting delicate edible ears. Except for bare brown arms, she was covered from top to toe in a white cotton affair which gave her no shape at all.

"Why, Mr. Preston," she greeted, half-smiling. "I didn't expect you quite so soon."

"There have been one or two developments," I told her. "I thought we might both benefit from a little conversation."

She pulled the door wider, standing to one side.

"Then please come in."

I stepped inside, and the fragrance of her was everywhere. She led the way into a large room where the furniture was scattered thickly, to give maximum freedom of movement.

"I was just about to have a glass of chilled wine. Will you join me?"

I was uncertain.

"Well — er — I don't know. In this heat — "

"I am not speaking of a heavy dinner wine," she explained. "This is a very simple affair from Greece. It is refreshing, not intoxicating. Unless you insist on drinking it by the gallon, of course."

"In that case, thank you, I'd like some."

Those Greek peasants would have been amazed to see their local brew being served up in the gleaming crystal goblet which was handed to me. I sipped at it, and she was right. It was light and fruity. Delicious.

"M'm," I acknowledged. "Very pleasant. I don't believe I ever had any Greek wine before."

She smiled, and there was mischief in it.

"They've been making it for five thousand years," she informed me. "In that time, a little expertise is hardly surprising."

There was no smart answer to that, so I merely smiled back. A man could do a lot of smiling around such a woman.

"You look hot," she said gently. "Why don't you take off your jacket."

Crazy world. I only put the damn jacket on to give my visit a touch of formality. Now, I slipped it off gratefully, and held it as I looked around for somewhere to park it.

"Let me."

She held out her hand, and as I passed her the coat, our fingers touched briefly. Something like electricity tingled up my arm. I thought electricity only travelled in one direction, but she dropped her eyes at once, so perhaps I was wrong about that.

"You Californians — " and there seemed to be a light tremble in her voice — "you never seem to adapt properly to the heat. The women especially. All they can think of to get them cool is to take off all their clothes. The Mediterranean people are much better adapted. This thing that I'm wearing is much more suitable. You'll find all the women in the really hot countries wearing some version or other of the same thing."

"It's very becoming," I assured her, "but I thought the idea in those hot climates was to keep the women modest, not cool."

She put the coat down on a chair. As she straightened up, the thin cotton clung to her briefly. Briefly, but long enough for me to be aware she was naked underneath. My mouth went dry.

"Modesty plays its part, naturally." She was standing close to me now. "I only put this on for that reason, when I saw who was at the door. Until then, I had been rather more — relaxed."

Meaning she'd been wearing nothing at all.

"I wondered about that," I replied. "I mean about your opening the door that way. A lady has to be careful these days."

"Oh, I am. As a matter of fact I've been rather frightened, alone here. But when I saw it was you I knew it would be all right. In fact," and she looked into my eyes, "I knew it was going to be all right from the moment we talked in your office this morning. I'll take that."

I was trying to get rid of the glass, although it was still half-full. Then the glass was gone, but she was back, only closer. Well, there was only one way to find out, I decided.

"You shouldn't have gone to all that trouble," I said softly. "Not just on my account."

She seemed somehow to sway towards me. My arms went round her as her head tilted back, and we came together. A moment later, she wriggled against me, and I felt material sliding past my hands. The cotton was a heap on the floor.

Stella Raymond was the same rich golden tan all over.

* * *

It must have been an hour later when I caught sight of the time on an ornate cherry-wood clock beside the bed. I stretched and yawned, enjoying my drowsy feeling. Stella's dark hair was spread over my chest, and I felt a protesting finger poking at me.

"Stop heaving about," she murmured.

I tickled her head.

"Don't you complain to me on the subject of heaving about."

179

She gave a throaty chuckle against me.

"Oh, I'm not complaining," she assured me. "Speaking as a client, I ought to tell you that I am quite a satisfied client."

"We aim to serve," I said smugly — and why not? Right at that moment I was feeling very smug. But that damned clock wouldn't go away. "Hey, I have to go."

"Go? Go where?"

She propped her head on one elbow and squinted along at me. She'd done it before, and knew the effect it was supposed to have. I'm used to making hard decisions, but this was the hardest yet.

"Out there," and I waved a hand. "I have to be where it's at, and that means out there."

"But I'm here," she pointed out, tracing slender fingers over me.

Three more seconds of that, and I would be a gone goose. I took a deep breath, cursed inwardly, and swung my legs over the side of the bed.

"Hey."

She collapsed, protesting, into the covers.

"I am a working stiff," I reminded her. "There's a certain lady hired me to get some action. That's what I have to go see to."

Stella hunched up on her knees, pouting.

"I would have said a certain lady was well pleased with the action, so far."

"Me, too, but unless you have Castanna locked up in a cupboard some place, then I have to go."

I went into the bathroom and splashed water on my face. She appeared in the doorway, and I was relieved to see she'd put on a dressing-gown. It was thin, but it was a covering.

"People seem to think Angelo Castanna may have murdered Burton Street," I said casually.

"Really?" she replied abstractedly.

"You don't seem very interested," I suggested.

She shrugged.

"I really don't see what it has to do with me. I'm not exactly au fait with the movements of waterfront riff-raff."

I shuffled about the place, picking up my scattered pieces of clothing and putting them on. "Street wasn't exactly waterfront riff-raff," I reproved. "In fact, he was rather a special man. He was one of your father's personal crew."

Bending to slip on a shoe, I watched her face out of the corner of my eye. There was a new hardening of the facial muscles, a sudden wariness.

"I didn't tell you about my father," she reminded me.

"Don't be so modest, Stella. You're a famous lady. You must have known I'd find out."

She nodded.

"Sometimes I wish I was someone else. Anyone else."

I could go along with that. If she'd

been someone else, then maybe — But she wasn't, I reminded myself.

"Didn't you know who Street was?"

"My father employs so many people," she hedged. "I may have seen him, even spoken to him. He'd be just another one of father's faces."

She was lying to me, and it brought a sour note into the air. That was foolish of her, to tell me that particular lie at that moment. I'd have been in the mood to believe almost anything she told me. Now, she was spoiling things. If it hadn't been for Darrel Street's visit to my office, I would have swallowed it.

"You wouldn't happen to know what they do for your father, these people he calls his personal crew?"

She shrugged, obviously wishing I'd change the subject.

"I haven't the foggiest idea," she said flatly. "My father, and his curious manipulations, are a source of total mystery to me."

"You make that sound as if you

don't care for him too well," I offered.

She looked at me then, with an expression I couldn't fathom.

"Care for him?" she echoed. "How could I? I scarcely know the man. You seem to have the family magazine concept of the term 'father'. People always conjure up this mental image of some jolly male figure who comes home at six o'clock every night and bounces the children on his knee. Do you ever stop to think what the word really means? All it means is that a man and a woman roll around on a bed for a few minutes, and as a result a child is born. That makes the man a father. That, and nothing else."

She might have been lying before, but what I was hearing now was the plain, bitter truth, and there was no mistaking it.

"He seems to have looked after you well," I remonstrated.

"Wrong. His staff looked after me. Nurses, governesses, lawyers, all kinds of people. They did it for money, which

184

is all most people understand. It's certainly all my dear father understands. Anyway, I don't want to talk about him. Why are you spoiling things between us?"

She looked suddenly defenseless and miserable. I took her in my arms and patted her, feeling like a heel.

"I'm sorry, honey, I didn't mean to upset you. I guess I've been in the business of asking questions too long. It's second nature to me."

She nodded, her head against my shoulder.

"Not your fault," she whispered. "It's me. The mention of that man always brings out the worst in me. Will I see you again?"

That, at least, was an easy one.

"Try keeping me away," I assured her. "You'll need two armed guards, as a minimum."

She looked up into my face while I was speaking, then turned her eyes away, almost in shyness.

"Despite everything," she said softly,

"I never quite lose this ridiculous fantasy. Some day a man will come along, and love me. Not my name, not my money. Just me. Childish, isn't it, at my age?"

"I don't think it's childish at all," I comforted. "Everybody has to have something to hang onto. This thing with us, who can tell? We'll need to give it some time. First of all, I have this job a lady hired me to do. I'll be in touch as soon as I can."

I kissed her gently, and she walked me to the door. As I was about to open it, she plucked at my sleeve.

"You will be careful, won't you? If it's true that this man already killed somebody, he'll be desperate, won't he?"

I laughed reassuringly.

"Don't worry. I'm the last person he'll want to harm. I'm the man with the golden arm as far as he's concerned. He wants money, not blood."

She nodded, wanting to be convinced.

"And you'll call me soon?"

"Next couple of hours, at most."

I went out then. The fountain was still playing, and the coolness of the little square made a fitting accompaniment as I walked reluctantly towards the harsh sun outside.

THEC7

10

FLORENCE DIGBY was on the point of going home when I reached the office.

"Oh, Mr. Preston, I'm glad I caught you. The telephone has never stopped ringing. Sam Thompson called twice. He seemed somewhat disgruntled at not being able to talk to you."

"Did he leave any message?"

"Not exactly. Last time he called he said you knew where he would be at six o'clock. Does that make sense?"

It did. At six, Sam would be back at his observation-post, watching a certain call-box.

"I'll catch him later. Who else called?"

Her expression changed to one of distant formality.

"Mr. Darrel Street. He's been

telephoning every twenty minutes, and he sounds rather distressed. In fact, he's about due again."

That didn't sound so good.

"Distressed? Did he say where I could find him? Leave a number?"

"No," she sniffed. "Mr. Street was not at all forthcoming. In point of fact he was quite rude when he heard you were out. As though he didn't believe me."

La Digby was offended. I grinned.

"I'll bet he believed you when you were through with him," I said, to mollify her.

Behind her the phone clattered.

"That could be him again now. Shall I — "

"No. You get off home. I'll see you in the morning. Did you manage to get that money stashed away?"

"Naturally. Good night, Mr. Preston."

As the door closed behind her I crossed to the desk and picked up the telephone.

"Hallo?"

"Zattu, Preston? Where in hell have you been?"

It was Del Street's voice, and Florence had been right. He did sound distressed.

"Where are you, Del?"

"I'm at Burt's place. Listen, I found something. You'll have to get down here right away. You have the address?"

"Why don't you just bring it to the office?" I demurred.

He almost squeaked in his irritation.

"Look, Preston, I don't wanta argue with you. This stuff I got here, it's dynamite."

Something had certainly upset him. He didn't sound anything like the man who'd been talking to me a few hours ago. There was something else, too. Despite the urgency of his words, the underlying tone was more of pleading than commanding. I didn't understand it. The police would have searched his brother's place, as a matter of routine, and I couldn't see them missing anything as important as Del Street seemed to think it was.

Well, there was only one way to find out.

"Be there in ten minutes," I answered.

He'd been right about Burton's having been no ordinary Jack-on-leave when it came to accommodation. The apartment was in a middle-price development of solid respectability. Location-wise it was only two blocks away from Conquest Street, where Sam Thompson would soon be taking up his post. Desirability-wise, they could have been a million miles apart. Ten minutes later I leaned on a buzzer on the seventh floor, and waited. The door opened a crack, and a quarter-inch strip of Del Street's face appeared. He nodded thankfully, and opened it wide.

I stepped inside.

"What's all the mystery?" I demanded.

"No mystery," said a new voice. "Get your hands up."

I turned, and there was a large forty-four looking at me. Behind it stood

Angelo Castanna.

"I might have known," I muttered feebly.

"The hands," repeated Castanna. "You carrying?"

"In my waistband," I confirmed.

"You, Del," he barked. "Take it out, and drop it. Careful now, or I'll kill the both of you."

Del patted around till he found the gun. Then he lifted it slowly out, and dropped it to the floor.

"All right. Inside."

Castanna stood clear, waving the gun impatiently. We marched through into the apartment as he bent down to scoop up my special.

"Siddown," he ordered. "Then we can relax."

Relax? He didn't offer any advice as to how a man is supposed to do that with a gun pointing at him. A gun which had probably killed once already. Street and I perched unhappily on the only two chairs. Castanna sat on the edge of the bed, watching us closely.

192

"Nice of you to invite me," I told Street sourly.

"Listen, Preston, I didn't have no choice — " he protested.

"That's right, he didn't," interrupted our captor. "I been wanting to talk to you, Preston. Lucky old Del dropped in."

"All right, so we're all here. What did you want to talk about?" I questioned.

Castanna's attitude puzzled me. In his position I would have expected him to be full of urgency and desperation. But he seemed almost at ease, and that made me anything but.

"You a smoking man, Preston? I could use a butt."

I tossed him an Old Favorite and we both lit up, staring at each other.

"Funny, the way things work out," Castanna said in a conversational tone. "Here's me, sitting around here, wondering what in hell I'm going to do next, when in walks old Del. You can imagine my surprise."

We both looked at him stonily.

"Yup," he continued, unabashed, "surprise of my life. I don't recall when I was ever so glad to see a man."

"You always stick up people you're glad to see?" I asked nastily.

He shrugged.

"Taking no chances, is all. Word is out I'm one of these desperate characters you read about. People don't take no liberties with guys like that. They just shoot 'em dead, and smile for the newspapers. What I'm doing here is like what you might call insurance. I have this thing about people shooting me."

"You and me both," I assured him. "But what did you mean about the word is out? You mean the word is wrong? Are you saying you didn't kill Burt Street?"

He made a dismissive movement with his gun-arm.

"Not the way they're telling it. We had a fight, Burt and me. It was him holding the gun, this gun. He was really gonna kill me, can you imagine? I didn't believe him at first, but he meant it all right. Then we had this fight, and the damned thing went off. I tell you, I felt sick."

Del Street stirred on his chair, and Castanna threw him a warning glance. I wanted to hear more.

"Why would Burt want to kill you?"

He looked cunning now, a man playing from a closed hand. It did nothing to enhance his attraction.

"Well, that's a long story, and I ain't got all day," he demurred. "But I'll tell you this. Burt and me was working for a very important man, the biggest. You can believe that or not, and I don't give a damn what you believe."

They don't come any bigger than Stavros Kurti, so I merely inclined my head in acceptance.

"So what went wrong?"

His mouth went very tight.

"What went wrong was Burt. He wanted to double-cross the big man, the number one. I never heard nothing so crazy in my life. A man might as well cut his own throat, and save everybody a lot of time. I mean nobody crosses that man, nobody. I tell you, even now, right this minute with every cop in town gunning for me, I won't even mention that man's name."

There was no doubting Castanna's fear of Kurti. It was unmistakably genuine. But that wouldn't stop him from telling me a tale, if he was out for some kind of deal. I decided to check him out.

"Let me tell what I already know," I suggested, "then you tell me what I don't."

"Maybe," he said suspiciously. "Let's hear it."

Del Street looked at me inquiringly. I nodded encouragement to him and started my tale.

"I know that you and Burt and another man went to collect something. This other man had ginger hair and a moustache, and that's all I know about him. I know Burt and you came back without that man. He seems to be missing, and there are people who think he's wandering around out in the bay with lead boots on. No, wait a minute — " as Castanna made to interrupt — "the thing you collected had to be valuable, and that's what this is all about. I think you and Burt took it, and now Burt is dead. That leaves you, Angelo. Tell me where I'm wrong."

He waved the forty-four impatiently.

"That's all crazy," he contradicted. "Well, most of it. There was this guy, I wouldn't call him exactly ginger, more fair-haired, but let it pass. We took him to a place, never mind where, and we came back here. Then Burt drives his car out in the desert. Burt has to wait and drive him back into town, kind of bodyguard."

"Why Burt?" I challenged. "Two bodyguards are better than one."

"That was the deal," he replied evenly. "I'm not supposed to get too

197

chummy with the man. Burt knows who he is, you see, but not me. Anyway, the next thing I know, here it is the middle of the night, and Burt turns up on the old *Eskay*, all excited. He's like sweating, you know, and he's got this little case thing like the business guys carry. I ask him what gives, and that's when he says the case is going to make us rich, and starts all this chatter about cutting ourselves in."

The part about Burt waiting out in the desert for me explained one thing. That bang on the head seemed to have come from nowhere, and now I had the answer. Burt Street had been in the back of the car the whole time. All he had to do was to wait till we got back, paste me over the skull, and walk off with the case.

"But the ginger man," I persisted. "Where does he fit in to all this?"

Castanna heaved his shoulders.

"He didn't. Burt said he wouldn't be bothering us any more. I figured Burt had let him have it."

"Crap," snapped Del. "Burt wasn't no killer. How can you sit and listen to all this stuff, Preston?"

I looked at him steadily.

"Two reasons," I told him. "One, Angelo here has the gun. When the man who's talking has a gun, I always listen. That's one reason. The way Angelo tells it is the way it shapes up. It fits the facts I know. That's the other."

He wasn't satisfied.

"You can believe what you like," he said grimly. "There's only one killer in this deal, far as I'm concerned, and that's him right there. He probably killed this ginger guy himself, and then shot Burt when he tried to prevent it."

"Listen, you," growled Angelo, rising to his feet.

"Wait," I said urgently. "If you two want to fight, leave me out of it. I only came here to get something. That's why you wanted me here, isn't it, Angelo?"

He stopped in mid-scowl, glancing from the wrathful Del to me, and making up his mind.

"You're right," he agreed. "The word is you're offering a whole parcel of money for this case. You have to be fronting for somebody. If it's who I hope it is, you have a deal. Right now. I was going to get the thing back to him somehow, no matter what. But with all this police hassle, I certainly could use those extra bills."

So that was it. Castanna assumed that the man behind the reward was Kurti himself. It was a natural assumption. For a moment I was tempted to go along with that self-deception, but at the last second I changed my mind.

"It's true I'm holding some dough," I affirmed, "but not for a man. It was a woman who came to me. The same woman Burt Street was rooting for."

His face fell.

"That's on the level?"

I nodded.

"She told me you'd already phoned her, offering to sell her the case. The price would be ten thousand. Is it true?"

His headshake was vigorous.

"True, nothing. I wouldn't have nothing to do with that party. Any case, I wouldn't even know where to reach her."

It was the kind of irrelevant detail which helps to underscore a statement. Castanna was telling me the truth. Stella Raymond had been using me, and I didn't like it.

"So we don't have a deal," I said softly. "What happens now, Angelo? It's your gun."

He waved irritably.

"Wait a minute, I gotta think."

"What kinda guy are you, Preston?" demanded Del. "Sitting around chewing the fat with this hoodlum. We oughta take him, is what."

"Calm down, Del. We're the losing team here. You want to go against that cannon, you're on your own."

This was no time for a fracas. To Del Street it was all very simple. It was just three men fighting in a room, two good guys, one bad. He didn't know about Hawkins and Kurti, and the massive forces involved in all this. I did, and what was worse, they knew about me. Whichever way things went, I was going to be the one responsible, and the knowledge did nothing for my peace of mind. I knew what people like that could do, and I knew they wouldn't hesitate to do it. If Street thought I was yellow, that was too bad. I wasn't specially afraid of Castanna, gun or no, but there were other people out there, and they were different. Hawkins, in particular. Like a bug on the wall was what he'd said, and he meant it.

"All right," announced Castanna. "It shapes like this. You and me, Preston, we go to see the man. You got no place in this, so you got no reason to tell him lies. He'll believe you, about the woman. I give him back the case, and I'm off the hook."

"What about the police?" I objected. "You won't be off the hook with them."

"Cops won't bother me, not once I'm square with the big man," he stated confidently.

I could believe it.

"Fine for you," I rejoined. "But after I tell my tale, what'll this friend of yours do to me? He won't like me, that's for sure. What happens to people he doesn't like?"

He grinned wolfishly.

"I'll speak up for you. You're just a cover-man, if you're telling it straight. If you ain't, he'll know."

There was the delicate question of Darrel Street.

"You think you can handle us both, once we get outside?" I asked.

Castanna shook his head.

"Not Del, I couldn't. He's got too much of the old seventh cavalry in him. He stays."

I got to my feet. Slowly, so as not to make him do anything impulsive.

"I won't stand for any killing," I told him.

"Killing? Who's talking about killing? I got nothing against old Del, here. No, we just kind of tie him up a little bit, keep him out of trouble for a while." Castanna stood beside the hapless Del, and rested the heavy forty-four against his neck. "If that's O.K. with you, Del?"

"Better kill me now, while you got the chance," gritted Street. "I'm gonna kill you, first chance I get."

Castanna's eyes widened in admiration.

"I gotta hand it to you, Del, you got plenty of the old moxie. To stay alive, you need a little more of that chicken blood. Like Preston, here."

I almost lost my temper then, and it would have ruined everything. But I kept my face turned away, while I looked around for things I could use to strap Del Street into the chair. Five minutes later we were ready to leave.

Castanna reached under the bed and lifted something out. I stared at the familiar shape of the briefcase which was causing all the trouble.

"Do you think you know how to open these things?" he demanded.

"No, I imagine you need a key."

"Key is right," he grumbled. "Some special key at that. Old Burt didn't keep any tools around, else I'd have had it open quick enough. I broke two knives on the damned thing."

I nodded, straight-faced, thinking of the damage that might have been done if he'd been successful.

"Must be something very valuable in there, if so many people are chasing it," I suggested. "I know a man who could open it in a few seconds. Then, maybe you and me could make some kind of deal. Could be a lot of money in it for both of us. Plus, I can offer you ten grand on top."

I was laying it on the line for Angelo. People talk a lot, but all they use are words. Show them the profit motive, the big fat cash bonus, and that's when you get at the truth.

Castanna shook his head, almost in pity.

"You don't listen very good, do you? You're giving me the same chatter I got from Burt Street. Only this time, I got the gun. Steal this, make a few grand, cut and run. All that jive. I woulda give you credit for more brains, Preston. There ain't nowhere in the world to hide from the big man. Ten grand on top, you say? On top of my tombstone is where. Now, cut out all that talk, and let's get outa here."

Del wriggled on the chair.

"Take it easy, Del," I advised. "You'll only make the knots tighter."

Castanna nodded approval.

"You done a good job there, I'll say that. C'm on."

I had done a good job, so far as tying up my ex-partner was concerned. It would have been a pity to spoil Angelo's good opinion by mentioning the clasp-knife I'd managed to leave inside the clenched fingers. Del Street should be free in an hour, or less if he got lucky.

Inside the apartment, Castanna had been quite cool and collected, very much the master of the situation. The change in him when we reached the street level was remarkable. His eyes were everywhere, his movements jerky. This was a man on the run, a man any policeman could use for target practice, and his whole body reflected it. Until that moment I'd been turning over one or two ideas about how to get the better of him, but that was changed now. This new Castanna was all ready to shoot anything and anybody. I walked slightly ahead of him and out into the dying sunshine.

On the steps outside, a group of men stood, chattering and laughing. They were all business types, and had evidently just broken up from some meeting or other. That's what I ought to be doing, I reflected sourly. Selling orange juice, or promoting computers. Something useful in life. I could have been one of those guys, not a care in the world, just swapping yams with my buddies. But not me. That wasn't my part in things at all. My job was to get down those steps without putting a foot wrong. Without doing the slightest thing which might cause the nervous man behind me to plant new holes in my back.

At the foot of the steps, a car door opened. A man climbed out, grinning at me. It was Hawkins, the man from the Internal Revenue Service. Damn.

"Well, well, Preston, we meet again — " he began.

"Duck," I shouted urgently, "this guy — "

Behind me, a gun went off, and a man shouted with pain. The crowd of businessmen was all around us. I was grabbed harshly from both sides. The shout had come from Angelo Castanna. He had been pulling the gun from his pocket when they grabbed him, and his finger must have tightened on the trigger. There was blood seeping through the leg of his pants as he struggled impotently against those steel arms.

He was cursing me in a loud voice, and the briefcase lay beside his feet. Hawkins walked round me and picked it up.

"Is this what all the fuss has been about?"

"I wouldn't know," I told him stolidly. "Has there been a fuss?"

He tapped me thoughtfully on the chest.

"You did yourself a good turn just now, when you warned me," he told me. "Don't go and spoil it by being difficult. Well, we mustn't stand around here chatting. Let's go somewhere more comfortable, so we can all relax."

As I climbed into the car I was trying to recall a time when I felt less relaxed.

11

TWENTY minutes later I was sitting on the visitor's chair at the imposing head office of Acme Toys and Games. Opposite me sat Hawkins, smirking enigmatically, and drumming lightly with his fingertips on a certain briefcase. I wished he wouldn't. I have this cowardly reservation about being blown to smithereens. The difficulty was, I was in no position to warn Hawkins that he was tapping at a potential bomb. My information on that had come direct from Kurti himself, and if Hawkins ever suspected I'd had dealings with the shipping man I'd find myself in the cell next to Castanna. Assuming he was in a cell. The last I saw of him, he was being helped into the back of a truck marked Tony's Ice Cream by three of Hawkins' hoods. Sorry, I ought to have said Hawkins' under-cover agents.

"Well, Preston, everything seems most satisfactory," beamed Hawkins.

"Glad you think so," I told him, without enthusiasm. "Listen, I might have been killed back there. Castanna was getting pretty jumpy when we came out of that place."

If the Revenue was concerned about me, he managed to conceal it very well.

"And I'm sure we're all very pleased that things turned out so well for you. It would have been unfortunate if anything had happened to you. It would have introduced a sour note into my report. As it is — "

He held up his hands, like an athlete acknowledging the crowd.

"I'm very happy for you," I said balefully. "I'd certainly hate to foul up your report by spilling blood all over it."

"Oh, tut-tut, don't make such a fuss," he reproved. "You've done very well, and I shall see that it is known in certain quarters. I wonder what's inside this thing?"

He pulled the case towards him, squinting at those locks. I cleared my throat nervously.

"I expect you'll need a special key to open it," I offered lamely.

His look was filled with cunning.

"Key? I'm not going to try any key. If this is what I think it is, it's practically a bomb. Perfectly harmless until you try to open it, then — blooey."

I hoped my enormous relief wasn't reflected on my face.

"Bomb?" I queried innocently.

"Exactly," he confirmed.

"I don't get it," I complained. "Are you saying you sent me chasing around the place, risking my neck, just to find a bomb? What are you trying to do, get me killed? What did I ever do to you?"

"Shush," he replied. "I won't let anybody hurt you. Besides, this thing won't hurt anyone unless it's tampered with. I had every confidence I could trust you not to do that. And it isn't just a bomb, as you put it. It's a self-destructive mechanism, and its main purpose is to destroy its own contents."

I could cut out the acting now, because my surprise was real. How did he know that?

"How do you know that?" I asked aloud.

"Seen one before," he replied triumphantly. "Istanbul. Three years ago. Identical piece of machinery. Unfortunately, that one worked."

This was no time for me to be asking what an Internal Revenue man was doing in Istanbul. Maybe there's an Istanbul in Tennessee.

"If you couldn't open that one," I pointed out, "what makes you think you'll do better now?"

He looked pained.

"Facilities," he replied, hurt. "Here at home we have facilities. Our people will work this out."

"Suppose they do, what do you expect to find?"

That brought a light frown.

"I don't know exactly, but it has to be valuable. Stavros Kurti does not concern himself with small details, and yet he personally interviewed the messenger, our Third Party, presumed deceased. That makes the contents extremely valuable."

"Something to do with this big swindle you were telling me about?"

"I imagine so. In fact, I'm almost certain of it. It's a pity the man Street got himself murdered. We were about to invite him in for a chat. Interesting man, our Mr. Street. He was one of a small band of people who worked direct to Kurti. People who never seem to be at their normal place of business when one of Kurti's ships comes to an untimely end."

I thought of the jersey, and the old *Monkton Pride*.

"A saboteur, is that what you're saying?"

"It's possible. However, there are others, once we can locate them. Uncle

Sam is preparing a massive and detailed block of evidence. It isn't a situation where the loss of an odd man here and there can upset the balance of the case. We've been working on this for years now. A few more months one way or the other will not really matter."

"Maybe the briefcase will provide all you need."

Hawkins shook his head.

"One doesn't expect miracles. This isn't some courtroom melodrama, Preston, where a surprise witness is tossed in during the last reel. This is a big operation. There are hundreds of pieces of evidence, thousands in fact. This is just one more, big though it might be."

It was all too much for me to absorb.

"Are you telling me you sent me out there, up against people with guns, for something which is only part of a jigsaw? A part you don't really need anyway? You say the loss of an odd man here and there doesn't matter.

Well, speaking on behalf of the odd man, I can tell you it matters to me. It matters like hell. I don't like you. I don't like you, and I don't like the way you operate."

If I sounded snappish and irritable, it was because I felt that way.

Hawkins didn't seem remotely offended. He sat back, hands spread out wide on the desk, and listened with no sign of rancour.

"I wish I could return the sentiments," he assured me, "but I can't. Fact is, for myself, I'm quite taken by your blundering, thick-ear approach. You were just the right man for this little operation, and the results are here to prove it. If you had been a shade more subtle, you might not have succeeded. You might even, and the thought horrifies me, have wound up in the same situation as the late Mr. Street. As it is, everything has turned out splendidly."

The guy was so imperturbable, I could only grin.

"Then how about a refund on my income tax?"

"Ah yes," he nodded. "Well, I don't get too involved with that kind of detail, you must understand. And, of course, there can be no question of paying for your services. After all, you have only acted as any right-thinking citizen should, in the best interests of the commonwealth."

The commonwealth was all very fine, but it doesn't butter my parsnips.

"I have this selfish interest in my personal wealth," I explained.

He lowered his voice in a conspiratorial fashion when he next spoke.

"Just between ourselves, I'll tell you what I'll do. You can make a substantial claim under deductibles for this little outing. Quote this reference beside it, and you'll find it will be allowed. Just the once, mind, and don't go passing it on to your friends. All that will get them is trouble."

I stared at the scrap of paper with the scribbled legend, and grinned. I was thinking of Florence Digby's face when I told her to make the entry.

Then I got to my feet.

"Well, If you don't have any more killers for me, or strange bombs to be located, I guess that'll be it. What'll you do with Castanna?"

Hawkins shrugged.

"I don't think he can help us very much. He's just another waterfront lout after all. We'll be turning him over to the proper authority for trial."

I hesitated before asking my final question, but I had to know the answer.

"And the man in the picture, the foto-fit character? Will you post him missing? You can't charge Castanna with his murder unless you can produce a body."

"Our Third Party? I'm afraid we'll have to write him off. My guess is that he's out there somewhere, a deep six citizen by now, but he doesn't really matter. This is what matters."

He patted at the briefcase.

I felt slighted to think of my missing

corpse being considered of such small importance, but this was no time to raise the point. This was a time to be leaving.

I shook hands with Hawkins, and got out before he thought of something else.

The sun was low now, and I was late making my call to Señor Ramondez. I stopped at the nearest pay-phone and pushed money in. After three rings a voice said cautiously, "Hallo?"

"Señor Ramondez?"

"Zattu, Preston? Listen, this is Thompson. Where in the Sam Hill have you been? I been chasing you all — "

"Calm down, Sam, I'll tell you later. Why are you answering the phone? Where's Ramondez?"

"He didn't show this trip. Listen, I followed the guy like you said. I thought I'd seen him before, but he was all done up in this hat and the shades, you know? Well, pin back the ears for a big surprise. Ramondez is a fake, and you'd never guess who he really is. He's Steve Raymond, the big entertainer, that's who he is. How d'ya like them apples? What kind of a — "

But I was no longer listening. It made sense, of course. Esteban Ramondez, Steve Raymond. Only a man as big as Stavros Kurti could expect a well-known character like Raymond to act as a go-between. The guy was his son-in-law, after all. Well, ex son-in-law anyway. At that moment I wasn't so interested in his identity as I was to know why he wasn't answering my calls. It was true I was late, but Thompson would have been covering from the agreed time. Something must have chased him off.

Well, it didn't matter any more. I only had one thing more to do.

★ ★ ★

An hour later I was leaning on the rail of Matt Newman's boat, staring at the huge, blood-red stain on the sea from the last rays of the sun. Matt hadn't been too enthusiastic about the trip, and only the prospect of getting a close view of Kurti's private yacht had persuaded him.

"He could've shoved off," he objected, but I didn't want to consider that possibility.

"I doubt that," I argued, with more conviction than I felt. "He has unfinished business ashore, and he has to keep close touch."

My sense of direction proved to be less reliable on the water than I was used to on land. We drove around a wide, sweeping circle, and finally Matt pointed.

"That could be her."

I squinted at the darkening horizon. Nothing.

"I can't see anything. Where aways?" I'd heard them say that in pirate movies.

"Right where you're looking," he confirmed.

"Fisherman's trick. You have to be able to focus on a sardine at five hundred yards."

"I could do that," I objected. "The sun would reflect from the can."

Then suddenly I had her. Low in the water, the yacht looked more powerful and sinister than I had remembered. We could turn back, I reminded myself. Kurti wasn't expecting me, and he'd never know I'd changed my mind.

True.

But then he wouldn't know what happened to the briefcase either. The case he'd paid me to safeguard. The first thing he would know would be when the opposition started using the contents against him, whatever they might be. All right, so the man was some kind of big-league crook, and he could fight his own battles. Why should I stick out my neck, my one and only precious neck, to help him?

Because you took his money, that's why, I answered myself. There was none of this social conscience chatter

222

then. All you saw was that big dollar, and you grabbed it. Now you owe the man.

My thoughts were as black as the engulfing night as we swung in close to the yacht. Suddenly, there were powerful lights shining out at us, and a voice with a loud-hailer.

"What ship are you?"

It seemed an elaborate word for Matt Newman's little launch. He looked at me to reply.

"Message for Mr. Kurti," I shouted. "Personal message."

"Stay where you are."

We rode on the gently chopping water while messages raced around on board the yacht. Then the loud-hailer shouted, "Come alongside."

Matt guided us neatly into position, and there was that snaky rope ladder again.

"Yours, I think," grinned Matt.

I swung and banged my way upwards, where burly arms pulled me over the side. An unfriendly face stared at me

223

from the other side of an automatic rifle.

"What's this about a message?"

"It's personal, for the boss himself," I insisted.

He bowed, insultingly.

"Who shall I say is calling?"

"Just tell him it's a man with a fair moustache."

I wasn't going to mention my name. There were a pair of ears on this ship that belonged to Hawkins, and I wanted no more to do with that man.

"You don't have a moustache," objected my new friend.

"That's right. But you tell him, just the same. And don't do this wrong, or he might not like it."

He stared at me for a moment, then barked at the men clustered around.

"Watch this guy."

He went away, and I waited. Newman's boat looked pathetically small, bobbing around below. It wasn't long before the man was back, and beckoning me to follow. We did that corridors and doors routine again, winding up in front of the same bodyguard as I'd seen on my last visit.

"Where's the fair moustache?" objected the guard.

"I shaved it off while I was waiting. I'll explain it to Mr. Kurti."

He searched me for weapons before banging on that familiar door. Then I was ushered inside.

Stavros Kurti sat in the same position as before. It was as though we had decided to reshoot the scene.

"Who are you?" he demanded.

Of course, I realised. He had only — seen me the one time, and I had then been wearing the whiskers he had supplied.

"My name doesn't matter," I replied. "You decided not to mention it the last time I was here. You thought the room might be bugged."

His face cleared.

"Ah yes, that man. I recognise the voice. You have not done very well, as I understand. You have lost my property."

The words were spoken in conversational tones, but that took away none of their seriousness.

"I have done worse than that," I replied, keeping my voice even. "I almost had it back this afternoon, but someone else beat me to it."

"The name of this man?" he demanded.

"We call him Uncle Sam."

"I see."

He thought about this for long moments, while I grew steadily more uncomfortable. He probably intended that to happen. Then he spoke again, but very softly.

"I think you had better tell me exactly what happened, starting from the moment you left this cabin. And leave nothing out. Nothing."

I told him the story. On the trip, I'd been rehearsing it in my head. Juggling with it, to see if there was any way I could keep Stella Raymond out of the tale. But it couldn't be done. She, or her influence, came in at too many important stages. I was going to have to include her, to tell this man that his famous daughter seemed to be with the opposition. The only thing I could do was to omit what had happened between us. That had been between a man and a woman, and was nobody's business but ours.

Kurti listened with extreme care as I recounted recent events. There was nothing on his face to suggest annoyance, outrage, or even interest. When I finally stopped talking, he waited a few moments. Then, "Is that all?"

"That's all."

He banged a pudgy fist on the table.

"Good. Very good. You have done very well indeed, Mr. — er, just Mr."

I looked at him, wide-eyed.

"I would have said I'd fouled it up in just about every possible direction."

He positively beamed.

"Ah yes, but that is because you

only have part of the story. Sit down, sit down, and I shall tell you a little more. Not all of it, you understand. I never tell anyone everything. But a little more is justified, I think."

I parked on the only available chair, and waited expectantly.

"There is certain evidence vital to my case which must not fall into the wrong hands," he began. "Unfortunately, this evidence is known about by others. I have enemies, you see, and I knew there was someone close to me who was working against me. I had my suspicions, but I could not be certain. That was when I decided to involve you. I let it be known that a mysterious visitor would arrive, but I delayed until a short while before you came. In that way I could be certain there was no communication with the shore. I had the radio-room locked up, and there is no private equipment aboard. Any arrangements which were made about intercepting you would have to be last-minute arrangements. Those are always unsatisfactory. Make do and mend, as I believe you Americans say. There would be loopholes, and I would find them."

"But the briefcase," I butted in.

Kurti held up a hand.

"Wait, please. My daughter's sudden decision to go ashore, at that ridiculous time of night, confirmed my suspicions about her. Until that happened I had resisted all the evidence, found every excuse for her. A man does not find it easy to accept that his own flesh and blood can plot against him." He coughed, and shook his head. "However, I could no longer deny the facts. What happened to you after that was really rather predictable. Routine, almost."

Routine?

"Routine," I said aloud. "Listen, I got banged on the head, I could have been killed, more than once. You call this routine?"

He looked at me with much the same expression on his face as I'd recently seen on Hawkins'. They ought to get together, these two. They could rule the world.

"The fact is, you did not get killed," he returned blandly. "You are a man of some resource, which is why I employed you. Besides which, you were being well paid."

"For a job I didn't do," I reminded him. "The briefcase — "

" — is useless. A simple metal box. I'm afraid I misled you about the contents. Those valuable papers I mentioned have since been taken ashore by quite different means, and are now in the proper hands."

"And it isn't a bomb, either," I muttered, half to myself.

"Certainly not," he snapped. "Such a device might harm quite innocent people. I am not a monster."

I thought of Hawkins, and all his backroom scientists, anxiously hovering round the useless briefcase. It made me grin. Kurti nodded.

"Good. I see that your sense of

humour has not deserted you. Now then, about the money. You may keep it. You may not have done what I asked you to do, but you have done what I expected, and that is quite satisfactory. There is one other reason, also."

The news that I could keep the money came as such a welcome surprise that I almost missed the last part. Then I realised he was waiting for some kind of reaction.

"Other reason, Mr. Kurti? What would that be?"

"Your delicacy. Despite everything, and despite all the provocation you have suffered, you still tried to spare my feelings. That is a gesture quite outside our arrangement, and, believe me, I appreciate it."

I knew it had to be something to do with Stella, but I wasn't quite sure what he was driving at.

"I don't follow," I said cautiously. "I told you everything that happened — "

"No," he cut in. "Not quite, I think. You carefully omitted to mention that

my daughter took you into her bed
— oh, you shouldn't look so guilty.
She is a most attractive woman, and
I do not hold it against you. One
becomes accustomed to these things.
You are a well-built, presentable man,
and my daughter has only one reaction
to anyone in that category. If that
is a blow to your ego, I am sorry,
but it's best that you understand the
position."

I understood the position all right.
It would seem that the whole family
had used me, one way or another. A
man's ego has high days and low days.
This would have to count among the
latter.

Twenty minutes later I'd banged
and cursed my way down that lethal
ladder again, and Matt Newman was
heading for the shore. I was in no
mood for conversation, and sat grimly,
staring at the twinkling lights along the
coastline.

As we neared the beach, Newman
spoke for the first time.

"Preston, I never interfere in another man's business, but whatever you're up to, I should take care."

"H'm?"

I had half-turned towards him. Of course, I remembered. Matt knew nothing of what had been going on.

"This Kurti," he said gravely, "he's not just some rich foreigner. A man who lives off the sea hears a lot of things, and, believe me, there's nothing good to hear about that man. Right now he's in big trouble with our own government. If he wants you to do something for him, I'd steer clear. It's likely to be dynamite."

Dynamite.

"You could be right," I said non-committally.

You bet he was right.

I thought about Kurti and Sella. About the Street brothers, and little Angelo Castanna. I thought about the top government involvement. And I thought about a certain case which caused all the trouble.

All in all, the whole thing had been much as Matt Newman had said. A highly explosive case.

THE END